REMEMBER ME?

A Collection of Short Stories

Andrew Noble

For Vivian,
μέ αγάπη
και φιλία

[signature]

FEB'24

ARTHUR H. STOCKWELL LTD
Torrs Park, Ilfracombe, Devon, EX34 8BA
Established 1898
www.ahstockwell.co.uk

British Library Cataloguing-in-Publication Data.
A catalogue record for this book is available
from the British Library.

DEDICATION

For Florrie and all the gang, both past and present.

By the same author:
A Gem of a Story

ISBN 978-0-7223-4793-5
Printed in Great Britain by
Arthur H. Stockwell Ltd
Torrs Park   Ilfracombe
Devon EX34 8BA

1. THE PRUDENCE OF MISS BRIDGET

CHAPTER ONE

Miss Bridget could not decide. In fact, she could rarely make any decision or choice without a great deal of soul-searching and wrangling.

As it was, this was a simple decision about whether to take a half-pint or a full pint of milk to cover the next two and a half days before she would travel to Devon to visit a friend for a short break away. After all, she negotiated with herself, it wasn't as if there was a house full of people, like the enormous Rooney family three doors down, who would all be glugging away gallons of milk on cereals, or in endless cups of tea.

No, it was just herself to account for, and she had been quite content with that arrangement for a number of years. Why change now what suited her best? So with that thought in mind she picked up the half-pint of milk and joined the queue at the till in the supermarket.

For a relatively small town, there always seemed to be such a long queue at this particular till. The sign clearly said that customers with only three items or less would be served here, and yet it constantly seemed that people were apt to challenge this cardinal rule. This was the very case now, with a heated argument rapidly brewing at the counter between a middle-aged man and the teenage assistant. The whole scenario irked Miss Bridget, and she tutted quite loudly to illustrate this. The man paused, spun round as if his neck was elasticated, and glared at Miss Bridget. Seeing her surprised him instantly, as he had not expected it to be her who had delivered the tut.

Miss Bridget in turn stared back. First at the man, then at what he held in his arms, which by any means of counting comprised four items, and then back at his face. She said nothing, she just stared witheringly at him in such a fashion that he immediately became clumsy and embarrassed; and so, in order to save face, he just slammed his things on the counter and stormed out of the store, muttering about 'women of a certain age'.

"Good afternoon, Miss Bridget," said Gemma, the assistant. "Just the half-pint today, is it?"

"Indeed it is. I'm off to see my friend Amelia on Friday, and it would be a waste to take more than I need until I go," said Miss Bridget.

Gemma appealed to Miss Bridget, as she was one of those few youngsters in the town who, in Miss Bridget's opinion, had made a conscious effort to better themselves in the face of screaming adversity, meaning to not be a statistical unemployed mother by school-leaving age. Miss Bridget understood that sometimes these things happened, but she just couldn't come to terms with what she deemed the total lack of self-respect and ambition which resulted in such a statistic. Gemma was not like that.

Had Miss Bridget known what Gemma thought of her, then the opinion might have changed. As it was, Gemma had been familiar with seeing Miss Bridget around the town for almost all of her young life. It had often seemed to Gemma that wherever you went Miss Bridget was there – either in the long queue at the post office on pension-collection day, where a myriad of swollen ankles and mumbling complaints shuffled their way towards the counter, or at the bus stop outside the betting shop, which was often the location for some of Gemma's best late-night activity with a boyfriend of the moment. The thought of Miss Bridget knowing or seeing

4

this, or even sitting on the wooden bench by the bus stop, made Gemma smile to herself as she handed the change over, and she wished Miss Bridget a pleasant trip to visit her friend.

Miss Bridget returned the smile and thanked Gemma before turning and heading for the exit from the store.

There it was, that cold slap across the face by the wintry wind that had it been a knife would have cut your ears clean off in one swift slice. It made Miss Bridget's eyes water too, and for a moment she had to blink twice in order to be able to focus again on the busy street in the weak light of the late afternoon sun.

As she stood there, Miss Bridget became what would later be described as 'confused'. She didn't see it like that at all. It was more a case of déjà vu – or a flashback to times past. That was how Miss Bridget had preferred to refer to it.

She was waiting for her father to come out of the butcher's shop. It was, as butcher's shops go, a magnificent specimen of its type. There were shiny white tiles everywhere, and hanging in the window was an array of wildfowl, along with rabbits and a hare – all ready for Mummy to come along and buy for supper. She could almost taste it – a rich winter stew, with rabbit and all the vegetables which Father had grown in the garden. Where was he anyway? It was cold, and the light was beginning to fade. Mr Wade, the master butcher, reached into the window display and took four large chops from a tray. He then slapped them into the greaseproof paper that covered his large hand. He looked at Bridget, smiled and winked at her.

It made her giggle and even blush ever so slightly.

"Are you OK, Miss Bridget?" asked Gemma, who had come out of the supermarket, having noticed the small frame of Miss Bridget fixed to the spot for what had seemed just that bit too long.

"I'm waiting for my father to come out of the butcher's. I think we're going to have some nice chops for our supper," replied Miss Bridget with a sweet and innocent childlike tone, yet totally sincere.

"You what?" said Gemma, slightly laughing, but becoming mildly concerned, and not knowing quite how to handle this situation. It certainly hadn't been in the manual she had received along with her uniform when she had joined the supermarket. "What butcher, Miss Bridget? It's Beyond Boutique . . . and has been for about four years. You might see some mutton dressed as lamb, but no chops." And Gemma chuckled at her own joke.

Miss Bridget stared back at her, and for a moment was indeed – for there was no other word to describe it – confused.

All at once, Miss Bridget found herself looking not at a butcher's window, and smelling the sawdust which Mr Wade had always sprinkled on the floor, but now it was a ladies' boutique window, dressed with winter-warmer clothes and fashions of the moment, with lots of rich colours in wool and faux fur. No rabbits or hares were hanging up – they had turned into the collared edges of coats and thick scarves.

Miss Bridget muttered the single word 'bunny' and turned round to Gemma, who by now had slipped an arm round Miss Bridget's shoulders.

"Are you OK? Are you going to be all right going home, Miss Bridget?" asked Gemma, looking up and down the High Street for a familiar face, just in case.

"No, dear, I'm fine. I just forgot where I was for a moment, but thank you for asking," said Miss Bridget as lightly and mildly as she could, walking away in the direction of home. "I'll see you when I get back from Devon. Goodbye."

As she watched Miss Bridget bustle away from the bright light shining from the supermarket's main entrance, Gemma wondered for the first time if, in fact, Miss Bridget really was going to Devon, or did she just think that she was going?

CHAPTER TWO

One of the nicest things about Miss Bridget's small bungalow was the covered porch which protected the side door entrance to the property. If the weather was being nasty, as it was this day, then the porch provided shelter from the rain as well as the strong gusts of cold and unwelcome wind. One of the worst things about the porch was that the same gusts of wind also blew endless piles of dead leaves around the door.

Between taking her gloves off to get her house key out of her purse and parking her shopping cart by the door, and then needing to wipe her glasses free of the drizzle which the wind had blown in her direction, Miss Bridget was quickly losing her temper with herself.

It was such a frustration, and everything seemed to require double the effort that it had used to. The thing was, as a cruel twist, that nowadays she didn't have double the effort or strength to utilise. So every damned thing of every damned day was a strain as well as a struggle.

Just as she managed to get her fingers to the door key, she dropped it and it fell into the pile of leaves, which then blew in a dizzy circle around her feet.

Miss Bridget then did something which she very rarely did – she cursed. She swore, blasphemed, and after a moment even shed a small tear of pure frustration and impatience.

This was getting her nowhere fast. She thought to herself,

'Take a deep breath, calm now, and just compose yourself. There, that's better – now, where's that darned key?'

Following what had felt like a tough five-minute trial and assault course, whereby Miss Bridget had managed, slowly, to bend down and retrieve her key, then open the door with fingers that were numb with cold, and then heave her shopping cart across the doorstep and into her kitchen, Miss Bridget finally sat down with a thump into her armchair.

There was just the small table lamp to illuminate the living room, and only one bar of heat glowing from the fire, but Miss Bridget rarely had more than these two things on, since with it just being herself in the bungalow what was the point of more? That would just be wasteful. As such, the lamp made everything appear cosy.

There was a certificate hanging on the wall opposite to where she sat, and as Miss Bridget relaxed in the armchair her mind wandered, and all of a sudden the subject of the certificate on the wall was whistling away in the kitchen. Her brother, William, was always a happy whistler. It hardly ever got on Miss Bridget's nerves; she liked to hear him around the house, or outside tending to his garden. Always, though, there would be a tune whistling through the air from yesteryear, and she found it comforting. William had been invalided out of the Great War, when he had been in the wrong place at the wrong time, and had suffered the loss of his right leg, along with his favourite horse, while fighting on the battlefields of France. He was lucky to get home, although he hadn't seen it that way at the time, or for many years after. He had to go to a military hospital to get an artificial leg fitted, strapped around his body, checked and all sorts, just to make it possible to walk kind of properly.

Through all this tedium and stress though, William whistled. It helped the other lads who were there with him, all waiting for their turn to be fitted up with artificial legs or arms.

Miss Bridget was so proud of William. He had always been

her big brother – the one you could depend upon, the one who saw reason, and who always saw the good in people. Whereas Miss Bridget would always buy just enough food to last a day or two, or make do with leftovers, William always said they should enjoy life to the full. After all, if he had been spared in the war, and had managed to come through it all with a shiny artificial leg and a certificate of honourable discharge from the King, then why shouldn't they enjoy the best of everything while they had the opportunity? Miss Bridget was apt to be more on the side of economy and prudence, but she had to admit, when William arrived home with the best cuts of meat, or an excellent bottle of wine, she would be the first to savour the flavour. She would sit in silence with her eyes closed in ecstasy, while she let the very luxury and best quality of things envelop her senses. When they had been away on a holiday together shortly after William's wife had died, he had insisted that they take the best seats in the house for the Isle of Wight Players' production of *The Mikado*, and Miss Bridget, once she had given in to his wish, had to admit it had been worth it in order to have such a good view of the stage. William enlarged his repertoire of tunes to whistle, and for a long time after would include melodies from *The Mikado* as he went about his business, every inch 'the wandering minstrel'.

Those had been the good times, but one day the whistling had stopped. William was found in the garden by a kindly neighbour, who, having heard the whistling stop, had looked over the hedge to see William lying still in his vegetable patch.

It had been sudden, and for William a lovely way to go. However, for Miss Bridget things were never the same again, and the hollow void left in her heart and home never quite managed to heal. She would hear William whistling more often than she would care to admit to – but that was fine, it made her feel safe and cosy.

Happy memories!

* * * * *

She awoke with a startled yelp, as if from a deep sleep when someone shakes you quickly and shouts, "Wake Up!" Of course, nobody had done so, but that was how it had felt to Miss Bridget. She rubbed her eyes, and looked at the clock which hung above the electric fire. 'Seven o'clock? Goodness, it must be time for some breakfast.' Miss Bridget rarely slept later than this hour.

She went into the kitchen, plugged the kettle into the socket on the wall and sought out a piece of bread, which was then put into the toaster. Marmalade was taken from a cupboard, and the small cup which sat on its saucer on the counter next to the small side plate was given a splash of milk and a teabag in readiness for the hot water when the kettle had boiled.

The toast made, marmalade spread and tea made, Miss Bridget carried a tray with her breakfast into her lounge. Having made herself comfortable, she put the TV on for the morning news. Why these remote-control things didn't have bigger buttons to make it easier for the elderly to press she didn't know, but it was a nuisance. However, after several hard taps the TV came on.

There was something not right, and Miss Bridget couldn't quite place what it was.

Where was her lovely, smart, handsome and intelligent newsreader? She particularly looked forward to watching him every morning as he delivered the world news in a way which she was sure felt like he was talking directly to her. But he wasn't there – instead, it was some young couple arguing over the baby which screamed in its cot next to them. This was a soapy serial – one which Miss Bridget had watched now for some years.

Why was everything upside down?

As she sat there, Miss Bridget began to panic, just a little. She didn't like this feeling. There was nobody to ask what was going on.

After what seemed like an eternity, but in fact had been about forty minutes, the news announced itself on the TV, and Miss Bridget looked up and focused on the screen.

It was the main evening news. She hadn't woken up at 7 a.m., but instead at 7 p.m.

Only now did the penny drop – and Miss Bridget was glad for once that there was nobody in her immediate area who would have seen this farce unfold, and who would have laughed at her for being so stupid. She kept quiet – oh yes, she wasn't going to let slip on this one; she'd keep her mouth shut and tell no one. It would all be all right after a good night, and the comfort of her bed suddenly had immense appeal to Miss Bridget, so she got up and straight away went to bed, and snuggled down under her duvet, where she felt truly safe and away from any harm or threat.

CHAPTER THREE

The fact was, cold and simple, that while Miss Bridget was under the impression that she had maintained her full sense of independence, this was not entirely the case.

Since the loss of her brother some years before, Miss Bridget had been locked into a world of her own creation. What had, in turn, revolved around her with great care and compassion were the actions instigated by her nephew. He had quietly negotiated with social-services case workers, assessment people, and the combined workers from meals-on-wheels service providers and the small army of visiting carers. Thus far, everything had worked well. It had helped, of course, that all parties concerned with the care provision for Miss Bridget had managed to not only get along with each other, but to maintain the level of contact between themselves. This meant that at any given time people understood what was going on. It had the appeal of a rare scenario: when service providers all work together well, and for a common goal, i.e. maintaining the quality of life for Miss Bridget.

Miss Bridget had a limited awareness of all these plans in action. It has to be said that at times it was purely a case of selective hearing and understanding by Miss Bridget. If she wasn't keen on someone who 'popped in' for a quick visit, then she would not hesitate to make her disapproval known to the individual. The result of this was usually a phone call to the nephew, to 'bring him up to speed', and within a day or two Miss Bridget could be found beaming and twinkling from the depths of her duvet covers, as she giggled in pleasure at seeing her nephew stood by her bedside.

She assumed he had a key to her home, but in fact there was a key safe tucked away on a side wall of the bungalow. Miss Bridget, had she known about it, would have done her best to remove or destroy the thing. Nobody would get in without her say-so, that was for sure.

But what was becoming a regular and growing problem was the delivery of the meals on wheels. For one thing, Miss Bridget could not decide whether she liked them or not.

This was difficult, as on a day when she would think that she liked them Miss Bridget would be sweet and welcoming to the young man who delivered the food. However, on a day where she had no time for the meals at all Miss Bridget would be aggressive and vocally abusive. She had been so bad on one delivery day that the young man had left in tears, with the meal thrown sharply after him.

Miss Bridget had remained bursting with anger for the rest of the day, and when the carer woman had arrived Miss Bridget was still sat in her kitchen stewing with rage.

Then, on one day when the nephew arrived for a visit, he discovered a pile of meals-on-wheels boxes in the kitchen, all untouched by Miss Bridget for almost a whole week. Although she had tried to hide them behind a curtain, and inside her bread bin, the nephew had no trouble in locating them by their smell. This was TROUBLE in big letters, as it meant now that there would have to be another assessment, and a few hard decisions made. Miss Bridget would, for sure, be totally determined to remain in her own home. The reality was that this would not now be in her best interest. The challenge ahead was to convince her that there was another course to follow, for maintaining a level of care which Miss Bridget would both accept and, in time, warm to.

The actual rapidity of Miss Bridget's decline was evident to everyone apart from Miss Bridget herself. This in itself was the heart of the problem at hand.

The nephew had visited, viewed and checked many of the care homes in the local area. It might have been predestined (came under the heading of 'meant to be') or just simple old-fashioned good luck, but the nephew managed to secure a room for Miss Bridget in a small, privately run care home which had a capacity for no more than fifteen residents. This made the home feel warm, cosy and homely – all things which would appeal to Miss Bridget.

Except that it didn't appeal to her – not one bit – and Miss Bridget dug her heels in for the long-haul defiant struggle against not only the nephew, but 'that wretched woman' from the social services who had come to visit, and who had sat in Miss Bridget's lounge trying to glean the simplest of answers to the most straightforward of questions with absolutely no success whatsoever. Miss Bridget was having none of it, and had sat tight-lipped throughout more than one visit. Not even the nephew being present had made any difference; in fact, it had only hindered things further, as the glare Miss Bridget let loose on both the nephew and the social worker was full of mistrust, fear and a sad recognition of what she deemed to be pure betrayal.

It had taken a further six weeks for Miss Bridget to finally 'give in', as she had seen it, although the nephew, the doctor and even 'that wretched woman' had all gone to great lengths to paint such a bright and colourful picture of how lovely things would be in the care home that 'giving in' had seemed quite the wrong term to use.

Finally, she agreed to go into the home for one week – just to see how it was. But, at any time, if she was unhappy, she would turn straight around and march out of the place, and return home. She had made it abundantly clear to everyone that this was her main condition, and they had all agreed unreservedly – perhaps a bit too quickly, but Miss Bridget was by now sick and tired of yet more struggling against what she had said was a challenge to her basic rights.

Anyhow, on a Saturday morning when the slate-grey clouds hung low in the sky, and the hanging baskets either side of the front door were swinging in unison, she was presented by the nephew to the manager, owner, and other residents at the care home.

'It is clean,' thought Miss Bridget, 'no dust or cobwebs, and a good-quality carpet too.'

There was the comforting aroma of a freshly prepared lunch wafting from the kitchen, and there was a gentle hum of conversation coming from the lounge at the end of the hallway.

Having been invited to have coffee and biscuits and to choose what she would like for lunch from a menu card, Miss Bridget very slowly sat back in the armchair which she had been guided to.

As she looked around, she noticed three people whom she had known years ago – one of them, in fact, she had even been in the same class with at school – but that was too far in the past to recall properly, and it was fuzzy and distracting to try and remember names and places.

If – and it was a big if, Miss Bridget decided to stay here, then she might choose to get to know some of these familiar faces, but for the time being she would do the same as she had done at home, and sit quietly, comfortably and warmly; and in between dozing off for a nap or two she would dream of happy visits to sunny Devon, whistling William, and Mr Wade's shop window. All that dead meat on display!

Miss Bridget looked around the large and airy lounge, and laughed out loud in such a way that, opposite to where Miss Bridget now reigned from on her new throne, Elsie jumped in her chair, and became tangled up in her brightly coloured knitted blanket.

As she looked at it, Miss Bridget thought that she might get one of those nice blankets for herself – and almost immediately she could hear William telling her, "Go on, you can afford a better one than that!"

2. TEMPERANCE:
Joey's Restraint

CHAPTER ONE

Joey looked in the mirror and liked what he saw.

Everything was just right – not too much here and just the right amount there. It was all there for the taking, and he'd be sure that tonight he'd get taken, hopefully by that pretty little blonde from behind the bar in the Crown and Anchor. He'd had his eye on her for a while now, although, for all the bravado and gusto which Joey exhibited in front of his pals and shipmates, he was shy and quiet when it came to the ladies. His mother had raised him to always be respectful to ladies.

Joey had been one of seven children, born and raised in a boisterous and loud suburb of a major shipping port on the south coast. School had been a semi-event in Joey's life, since he had been keener on daydreaming, and he would gaze endlessly out of the classroom window towards the horizon outside the harbour wall. Whatever dreams lay beyond it had far more appeal to Joey than the sums being scrawled on the blackboard.

Being the youngest of the seven children in the household, Joey had learnt early on that if you wanted something, or at least a chance of getting something, then you had to be prepared to fight for it. He learnt very quickly how to fight, and became rather good at it. To this end, Joey always managed to get food from the serving dish onto his plate, and always managed to get a warm blanket for himself at bedtime.

Having left school without any great expectations or qualifications, Joey found work as a bookie's runner, and could be seen racing around town as fast as the winner in the 4.30 at Cheltenham. He was reliable, and would always return to the bookie with his pockets bursting with money and betting slips handed over by many sailors who had fancied a bet as soon as their ship had docked in port.

It followed that, in the course of time, Joey had been able to apply, and achieve, a position on a mailboat. Not the highest of ranks, but, as his mother had said proudly when she saw him off at the docks, "Everyone has to start somewhere, and travel broadens the mind." She was relieved that he had made it onto the boats, and although he was not a fully fledged Royal Navy seaman, a merchant seaman on the Union Castle line's run to Cape Town or Buenos Aires would do nicely.

Joey was just happy to be able to now go beyond that horizon which he had dreamt of for so long.

He had enjoyed the travelling, and the adventures of visiting exotic places, where you could smell the scorched earth after heavy rains, and where rum cocktails were poured by sultry and bronze-skinned women in bars that carried the salty air of being dockside, as well as the tales from faraway lands.

Brightly coloured flowers matched the vibrancy of local costume, and Joey would return home with scarves for his mother and sisters, and cigars for his brothers and father. They had all been agog with interest, and had all sat in a stunned silence round the dinner table when he had returned once with a fresh pineapple and a noisy parrot.

The pineapple had been devoured for supper, and it had only been pure luck that the parrot got sold on, and had not joined the pineapple on the dinner table.

So, now that he was on shore leave, Joey was determined to make up for lost time. He had managed to get a light tan, which had improved his general complexion from that of the milky-white local boys.

His previously skinny frame had filled out a bit, making him look trim, neat and slender rather than skinny. His short hair, with a side parting that you could roll a coin along, was shiny, dark and, like his figure, neat.

He had clapped some cologne onto his cheeks, and snarled at his reflection, checking his teeth were clean and dinner-free. Clean handkerchief in pocket, money in wallet, cigarettes in breast pocket, all checked.

With a happy cheerio, Joey walked the short distance to the Crown and Anchor, paused briefly outside to take a deep breath and, flinging the door open by its long brass handle, made his entrance.

Evie had the most beautiful hair. Everyone had said so ever since she had been a small girl. The thick long golden mane hung over her shoulders and curled itself in all the right places, framing her face and neck perfectly as well as naturally.

"Mind you," as she would always tell you, "this doesn't just happen by itself, you know. It takes a lot of time and effort to look this good."

Most of the young men in the district fully appreciated the work that had gone into Evie's presentation. They had all at various times made a play for her. The young man from the fishmonger had tried, but Evie had taken one look at his fingernails, and 'Really? I don't think so' became her motto not only for the young fishmonger, but for all the others who had tried and failed.

There wasn't a lot to Evie. She was small in stature, and had a decent, full figure. She made up for being, as the lads called her, 'pint-sized', by being quite loud, and would laugh at almost anything.

She had often wondered where Joey was – she knew he had been at sea. Now, having caught him on her radar, she struck up an across-the-bar conversation. He mumbled, blushed and dropped his change. Having seen him blow into the bar like a tornado to see his chaps, Evie was enthralled that she could

19

have this effect on Joey, and as she eyed him up and down she noted that he had improved over the past year or so.

It was while Evie was giving Joey what she and her gang of girly friends called 'the total up an' down', someone else, curled in the corner of the bar among the shadows and beer stains, was doing the very same thing to her – except he wouldn't have called the look anything as mild as Evie had termed it in a flourish of giggles with the girls.

Dickie was, at best, someone you might think of as a 'have a go' sort of fellow – but with a distinctively unsavoury undercurrent coursing through him. The world, as he saw it, owed him. Permanently.

Therefore, it was his right to take what he considered he not only deserved, but had a right to have. No discussion, no issues raised, it was as straight as that. This, in effect, was the only straight thing about Dickie, for in every other way he was selfish and twisted. People who knew him avoided him, and would pass on the other side of the High Street.

While doing so, they would share the line that "He's a real bad penny, and will end up on the end of a rope one fine day, you mark my words."

Those who didn't know Dickie would soon reach the same conclusion after he had taken them for a day at the races, and introduced them to his circle of friends. After a wonderful afternoon's racing, for Dickie and his circle at least, the poor victim would board the train home, so stunned at his loss of fortune that he would be sure to miss his footing upon the step into the railway carriage.

Dickie liked Evie. She had no time for him, other than to perform her job and serve him his drinks across the bar. He was a customer, that was all. She was the one everyone liked, wanted or wanted to be. He was determined that tonight she would be taken by 'Dancing Dickie'.

While Joey fished in his pockets for some money which hadn't rolled away across the floor like a lost dream, Dickie emerged from the safety of the shadows and stood shoulder to shoulder with Joey in front of Evie.

As Joey was about to apologise to Evie for keeping her waiting for his money, Dickie flashed a crisp ten-shilling note. He waved it in between Joey's nose and Evie's face on the other side of the bar.

"Stick a large one in for me, doll," sneered Dickie, enjoying the jerked recoil of Joey's nose from his clenched fist holding the banknote.

'That'll sort him out and keep him away,' thought Dickie as he waited for the drink, and lit a thin cigarillo.

Now, Joey, even when on his best behaviour, had always had issues with self-control. Dickie knew this only too well from the playground days of old, back at the school they had both attended; nonetheless, he was keen to exploit the situation.

Joey didn't take kindly to having a fisted ten-shilling note thrust under his nose, especially when the complete disrespect attached to it belonged to Dickie, and was destined for Evie. This was a double no-no, and would have to be addressed. He couldn't resist the urge. So, without any further hesitation, Joey raised a large weathered hand and smacked Dickie's fist to one side.

"It's rude to interrupt, especially when Evie here is looking after me."

"Is that so?" smiled Dickie thinly. "Well, best she sees you for what you are – a bully with a short temper. I'll even bet you didn't get callouses like them on yer 'and from just swatting flies in Buenos Aires."

Joey didn't flinch. He knew Evie was watching him – he could feel her eyes boring into him, imploring him not to take Dickie's bait. It would let her down if he did, and then that would be that. Evie's girls would make sure that she never, ever again had the chance to spend time making a play for Joey.

Evie stepped forward to the bar top, put Joey's beer in front of him and scooped up the small pile of coins from the bar towel on the counter.

"Go and join your mates, Joey," she said carefully and slowly, making sure that she held his gaze.

After what seemed like an age, but, of course, was in fact just a few seconds, Joey did as he was bid. Taking a large gulp of his beer, he turned and went to where his mates were making plans for a darts game.

Dickie, had he been a rooster, would have crowed. As it was, he brayed a long drawn-out laugh which poured scorn at Joey's back. The tops of Joey's ears went crimson, but he didn't turn.

CHAPTER TWO

As much as Joey's pals tried to divert his attention away from the background chatter that Dickie was employing to try and secure an after-hours date with Evie, they were failing miserably.

Yes, Joey was pleased to see them; they were a merry little group who had stuck together since they had all played in the backstreets after school. They all knew each other well, and, as a group, they all knew when Joey was beginning to crisp up, given the high intensity of his own self-roasting in this atmosphere. He threw his darts with such malice that it was a miracle that the board remained intact, and had not splintered before them all.

Joey's scores were not at his usual competitive level, simply because there was something more competitive for his mind to be wandering back to.

As the pub's landlord rang the large brass bell above the bar and bellowed, "Time, gentlemen, please," Dickie hopped off his bar stool in the corner and meandered slowly through the crowd towards the toilets, which were outside, through a frosted-glass door at the end of the bar.

Dickie slowly pushed the toilet door open with one finger and peeped around the corner before entering the cold, damp and less than clean pub toilet.

Stood at the urinal, legs apart, yet still swaying ever so

slightly, was the large bulky frame of a man that was named Stan. He had been for some time a co-conspirator of Dickie's, and was not in the habit of being delicate or diplomatic with any 'mark' that Dickie had managed to work his nasty spells on. Therefore Stan had his uses, and as he wasn't the sharpest tool in the box Dickie found it easy to manipulate him.

As Dickie washed his hands, or at least made a veiled attempt at doing so, Stan tidied himself and stepped down heavily and clumsily from the urinal.

"So, are we still on for Saturday?"

"Of course we are, Stanley boy," sneered Dickie. "I've been lining this one up for a few weeks now. . . . He's almost putty in me 'ands. When you see his smart Savile Row suit, and hand-stitched leather shoes, you'll know he is ripe for the picking clean – yeah?"

"Yeah," leered Stan, letting loose a small amount of dribble, such was his controlled excitement at the prospect of not only fleecing a 'mark' again, thanks to Dickie; more tempting was the possibility of beating the stuffing out of the 'mark' afterwards if he didn't cough up for Dickie. That was what Stan always enjoyed most, and he said so. "Don't forget, Dickie, if he don't pay up, I can 'elp him see things our way, even if he breaks his legs or arms in the process."

Dickie smiled and patted Stan's shoulder. "Now then, Stanley boy, control yourself. We don't need another close call like we had last month. I mean, Stanley, I know I said we should get him to see the light of things, but I didn't mean you should help him fall in front of that train."

Stan stepped back, and for a moment became embarrassed with himself. "You know I didn't mean that to 'appen, Boss. It was an accident. He just lost his balance and fell backwards . . . right into the pathway of the train."

Dickie sighed. "Oh well, it happens like that sometimes. We can't win them all, and we were lucky that there was nobody around at that time of night to see anything. . . . It was just another suicide for the fuzz to write up. Now, get off out of here, and I'll meet you at the usual spot on Saturday. I'll call upon Mr Gerald Hartley at his Esquire Club in Piccadilly tomorrow, and dangle the final juicy fruit of a bet that can't fail with him."

Stan strolled out of the toilet with the air of someone who had just received absolution in a confessional box, and who was ready to repeat the sin seeing as how it had been so easy to get forgiven for it the last time.

Dickie was about to light a cigarillo, and linger a minute or two before leaving, when the lock-up cubicle door opened and Joey emerged into the dimly lit floor space between the urinal and the wash-hand basin.

"That was pretty slack, even by your standards, Dickie," said Joey.

"I didn't think anyone was in there," mumbled Dickie. "I thought you were still outside playing darts with your girlfriends. Still, these things happen. Now, I have an appointment if you don't mind."

Dickie tried to make a move towards the toilet door, but before he could take more than two or three steps Joey had leapt forward, grabbed Dickie by his lapels and pinned him to the wall.

Joey's body trembled with the electrified anticipation of a caged animal which, realising its captors have left the door open, has come out looking for blood and vengeance.

"I think it's about time I taught you a lesson," barked Joey. "You're long overdue a bit of Joey's attention, Dickie boy."

Dickie, on realising he wasn't in the best of positions given the situation at hand, lost his cool. "You can't touch me, Joey – I'll have you up for assault in a jiffy."

"There's just one thing," smiled Joey: "no witnesses. It's just a station platform late at night, nobody around."

With that, Joey launched a punch that made perfect contact with Dickie's nose.

CHAPTER THREE

As was the case with most pubs, the final half-hour had been a madhouse as far as the bar was concerned, and the till was ringing with the happy merriment of a Christmas carol.

For the first time in a while, Evie paused. She took a sip of her Martini and lemonade and looked around the bar for Joey. She couldn't see him, and her heart sank. Surely he hadn't left without as much as a goodbye?

She took a cloth and went around tables clearing glasses, and emptying ashtrays into a bucket.

As she got to the table where Joey's pals were putting their coats on, and drinking the last gulps of their beer, she asked where he had gone. They nodded towards the toilet and smiled.

Evie was relieved that Joey hadn't left yet, but this relief evaporated as she soon realised that Dickie was also nowhere to be seen. She should check, just to be on the safe side.

Evie needed an excuse, so, with ash bucket in hand, she marched into the men's toilet just in time to see Joey land his second punch just above Dickie's right eye.

She let out a small cry: "Joey! No."

In fairness, both Joey and Dickie were surprised to see Evie stood in front of them, there in the men's toilet of the Crown and Anchor. It gave Evie the moments she needed.

"Please, Joey, put him down. He's not worth it. He's been on at me all evening to go off with him for a nightcap cocktail somewhere, but I ain't going. I want to be with you, Joey. I want to hear about your adventures. I want you to share with me what it's like over the horizon."

"You what?" said Joey. "Did you just say 'horizon'?"

"Yeah – I always wondered what it was like to go beyond the horizon, and I can't think of anyone better to do it with," Evie said, full of self-pride, but tinged with a hint of shyness.

Joey sighed. He couldn't cope with two things at the same time, especially of this magnitude. So, with a sudden drop and slump, he cast Dickie to the floor like a rag doll and wrapped his arms around Evie. This was a far better place for his arms and hands to be, and he knew it instantly.

He looked down at Dickie. "I think you had best make yourself scarce from around here, don't you? I don't mean for a week or so either. And take your gorilla with you too."

Dickie merely stared back through the eye that wasn't starting to swell up and gave a short, curt nod.

Evie, in a gesture of finality and triumph, emptied the ash bucket over Dickie's head and dropped it on the floor next to Dickie's now stained tweed trousers.

"There," she said sweetly, "ashes to ashes, dust to dust!"

Joey and Evie walked along the lane that led from the pub by the docks and up a hill, from where they could see beyond the harbour wall.

"Just a tick," said Joey, and he went into a telephone box.

Evie stood outside, looking up at the stars that twinkled down at her. Pursing her lips, she blew curls of hot breath into the chilly night air. What was he up to in there? He was on to his second call now. . . . Good grief!

Joey emerged a minute later with a small smile on his face. "Sorry about that, babe. I just had to call a friend at the Esquire Club in London."

Evie giggled. "The Esquire Club? That sounds real fancy, and a long way from the Crown and Anchor! Who do you know there,

My Lord!" Mocking Joey, she curtseyed theatrically to him.

"Oh, it don't matter any more," said Joey. "Now, you, come here to me."

Having chased each other, and finally caught up together, it was without any effort at all that they cuddled each other closely. It felt so right. For all of Joey's restraint, it was only Evie's influence and gaze at the end of the day which could fully affect his self-control. After all, as his pals would say to him on his wedding day, "Dynamite comes in small packages."

3. HOPE:
Best Foot Forward For Elsie

CHAPTER ONE

"Oh, come on, Elsie! It's almost twenty past," Phyllis shrieked up the stairs as she stood in front of the hall mirror, adding the final touches to her immaculate self-presentation.

She almost purred with contentment as she admired how the light danced around the diamante droplets that hung from her dress. It was just a pity that the origin of the light was the singularly sad light bulb which dangled rather than hung from the ceiling mould in the hall. It wasn't by any stretch of the imagination a beautiful French chandelier in a Parisian salon; it was exactly what you would have thought it to be – the dim and damp hallway of a terraced house in the East End of London. Nevertheless, Phyllis had taken a lot of care and attention in the preparation of what she now inspected in front of the mirror. She was not tall, and no shorty either; yet with a slim and nimble figure, her dress hung perfectly from her shoulders. She had an oval face, to which the perfect amount of make-up had been applied. The fact that the make-up was comprised of a selection of gathered samples from London stores was not important – the effect was very satisfying. Her hair had been styled, waved, and now shone under the light bulb, but Phyllis knew, or rather hoped, that later on it would tantalise a nice young man with its golden radiance. A nice, rich young man.

Phyllis sighed. It was like this every darned time they went out. She looked at her watch and shrieked again, this time a pitch higher. "If you don't hurry up, Elsie, I'm leaving without you – and I mean it this time."

"All right, all right, I'm 'ere, ain't I?" squealed Elsie as she came downstairs, half running and half jumping.

"Well, I never!" gasped Phyllis. "You look amazing, but you'll have to remember not to drop your aitches, and watch out for a slippery 'ain't' too while you're at it. After all, where we're going we've got to keep up our appearances, and try to find ourselves a nice beau or two."

Elsie paused briefly in front of the mirror, and ran an eye up and down herself to check that everything was where it should be and looked fabulous. It was, and it did. Elsie had a slim figure like Phyllis, although thanks to her keep-fit exercises Elsie's shoulders were just that bit stronger. Her chocolate-brown hair had been cut into a pageboy bob cut, and this framed her bright face just right, showing off her dark eyes and button nose to the full extent of their cuteness. Elsie had learnt, a long time before, how to make the most out of being 'cute', and her elfin features seemed to enhance the daring, naughty giggle that she let escape while she paused to untangle a droplet earring from the undercarriage of her hair. Then, wrapping herself in her full-length fur-trimmed orange silk wrap, she hurtled out of the front door ahead of Phyllis, and the two 'best friends' raced along the street, laughing and panting as they ran for the bus.

What they always did on such an evening out was to take the bus so far, then the Underground a bit further in, and then, for the last bit of their journey into the bright lights of Piccadilly and Mayfair, they shared a taxi together, so that on arrival outside the Tivoli Club in Dover Street they could be seen to arrive in something more upmarket than London Transport could provide.

"Don't forget," whispered Elsie as they approached the entrance to the club, "it's Elsie, not Else!"

"Oh, absolutely, darling," replied Phyllis, who was almost breathless with excitement. "And as for me, call me Phyllis, not

Phyll. That way I won't sound like the Victorian spinster of an aunt I was named after. She lived in Kent and played too much golf for her own good. Phyllis sounds more fun than plain and dull Phyll."

With that, and in a clutch of giggles, the two young ladies remembered the way they had seen Ginger Rogers glide onto the set in a film recently, and went through the revolving door of the Tivoli Club.

'Optimism and hope are in the air,' thought Elsie to herself, and as she dropped her shoulders to let her silk wrap slide down, to be left at the cloakroom, there was a definite intention that tonight would be the night. Phyllis might find the whole experience a bit of a laugh and a giggle, a dare even, and any chance of an encounter was just that – chance. But Elsie fully intended to elevate herself out of East London drudgery, and find a nice young man to make it happen. Yes, tonight's theme was *possibilities*.

It was with this word in mind that Elsie perched herself on a stool by the bar, and Phyllis ordered two Martinis. The hours spent in the cinema watching a selection of Hollywood sirens floating all over the screen had all been absorbed with intensity by the two friends; and if you were to cast an eye along the bar in the Tivoli Club that evening, the two young ladies sipping their Martinis, playing carefully with their olives on cocktail sticks would have caught your eye amid all the buzz of the club. In fact, you could have been forgiven for thinking that it was Jessie Matthews and Ginger Rogers sat there sharing drinks and a few stories together.

It would be fair to say, without exaggeration, that on this night in particular the Tivoli Club was absolutely hopping with vibrant activity. There was not a free table or chair to be had, and the dance band was in full flow. People were dancing on the small dance floor, seemingly delighted that, due to space constraints, they HAD to be squeezed closely to each other in order to rotate around the perimeter of the floor, and keep up with the intoxicating rhythm of the band.

After a ten-minute run of some exciting jazz music, which had in recent years crossed the Atlantic on liners from the edgy clubs of New York, things calmed down a little. A singer took her spot in front of the band's conductor, and proceeded to sing the new song by Mr Cole Porter. People took their seats and ordered cocktails, while a few diehards remained on the dance floor, almost lazily swaying to the melody of the song.

Elsie and Phyllis were swaying ever so slightly, so pleasant was the tune, and they completely missed the two young men who came to the bar beside them and ordered champagne.

"We'll take four glasses," one of the chaps said, and his pal swallowed a giggle as, without hesitation, two of the glasses were placed before the two young ladies.

"You will join us, won't you, girls?" said the shinier of the two young men to Elsie.

His jacket lapels were shiny, his oiled and brushed-back hair was shiny and his cheeks and nose were shiny too, although, to be fair, this was more to do with the fact that thanks to the dancing and crowds it was becoming stiflingly hot inside the club.

"Go on, have a glass, no strings attached. I'm Ernest, and this is my pal Freddie. We've just got in from Le Touquet, so it seems a shame to stop the champers now, right?"

Elsie slightly raised a pencilled eyebrow and stole a glance at Ernest over her shoulder. She'd seen Fay Wray do it in a film only last week. It had looked so glamourous, and yet held full control over the male at hand. Lovely!

"I don't mind," she replied casually. "Besides, I can't bear to waste a drop of the good stuff. This is Phyllis – say hello, Phyllis! – and I'm Elsie. Charmed to make your acquaintance!"

She trilled a light laugh, more from a flutter of nerves than anything else. Having taken one glass, which Ernest had already filled, she passed it to Phyllis; then she curled a finger round the stem of the other glass, which Ernest was pouring. She gave

Phyllis the smallest of nudges with her knee as she crossed her legs, pointing a toe in the direction of poor young Freddie, who was stood like a lost child in a department store at Christmas. Phyllis took the hint, and, with glass in hand, she headed over to where she and Freddie began to chat about how bored the singer looked, considering the quality of Mr Porter's song.

"So were you in France for long?" asked Elsie, sipping her champagne as if it was piping hot.

"We like to go for the season," said Ernest, "but at least twice during the run we get called back for a wedding or some other function here in town. One can't say no to things like that."

"No," mused Elsie, "I don't suppose one can."

CHAPTER TWO

It hadn't taken long for the Martinis and champagne to have an effect, and soon Elsie and Ernest were dancing together, and swaying in rhythm to the sound of the band as they played 'The Continental', which was one of the most popular tunes of 1934.

"This is my favourite tune of the year," said Elsie as she flashed a smile over Ernest's shoulder in the direction of the bar, where Phyllis and Freddie were now thoroughly well defrosted and enjoying a relaxed laugh together.

Phyllis returned the smile to Elsie, and both parties were pleased to be in such pleasant company.

"Have you seen *The Gay Divorcee*?" Elsie asked, trying to sound as upmarket as she could, so that the word 'Gay' came out as 'Geh'.

Ernest looked slightly quizzically at her for a moment, before answering. "Yes, Freddie and I usually try to get to the pictures as much as we can – we like to see the Pathé News feature as well as the main picture."

The band finished their song, and a short interval was announced. Ernest, being the complete gentleman, escorted Elsie back through the crowd towards the bar.

It was as they were between tables and chairs that she saw them. She had to strain her eyes a little to be sure, but yes, it was – and here of all places. . . .

'Fancy!' she thought to herself.

She quickly picked her way through the crowd and arrived squarely in front of Ernest and Elsie, bringing them to an abrupt halt.

"I thought it was you! Didn't you see me wave from over there? I s'pose not, what with this one in your arms keepin' ya busy. What are you doin' 'ere, you devil? It's not your usual haunt, is it?! I'd have thought you'd be in The Red Lion with Fred. How's yer mum?"

Ernest just stood there, rooted to the spot by his embarrassment. He had no idea what to say, and, even if he had, his mouth now felt so dry that his tongue wouldn't work.

So, with a hand thrust forward, Elsie introduced herself. "Charmed, I'm sure. I didn't catch your name."

"Oh, it's Ivy – an' don't worry, ducky, I've known Ernie 'ere for years. We were at school together in Bethnal Green, weren't we, Ern?"

Ern nodded in such a way that had it been speech it would have had rather a severe stammer.

"I must get on – I've only got ten minutes to get round this place and sell as much as I can from this thing." Ivy clucked, looking down, and rearranged the assortment of goodies in the box which hung round her neck on a broad ribbon. It seemed to Elsie quite appropriate that Ivy should have such a ribbon around her, since it made her look just like one of those large dolls that rich little girls got for Christmas and took with them for tea at The Ritz.

'Except', thought Elsie, 'I've never been to The Ritz, and from the look of it neither has young Ernest here.' She placed a hand in the small of his back and steered him forward, circumnavigating their way around Ivy as they went.

"Well, it's been lovely to meet you," Elsie lied. "No, I don't think we want anything from your tray of goodies, but thanks all the same. Come along, Ernie." With that she guided Ernest into the boisterous and jostling crowd which was halfway between the bar and the dance floor, where the band had returned to their seats in preparation for their second half.

"Look here, please don't say anything," pleaded Ernest, trying to sound as sincere as he felt, which didn't really work as his words fell out of his mouth in a quick tirade of squeaky guilt. "Honest – I really like you, and I know Freddie over there is having a lovely time with your pal, so why spoil it all?"

"Because," Elsie hissed, "it's all a big fat lie, isn't it? France indeed! I bet the nearest you've been to France is that cake shop in Soho that does the fancy stuff."

"What if I have?" barked Ernest, feeling somewhat under attack.

Then all of a sudden his head cocked to one side a little, and he stared at Elsie for a lingering moment. She was a pretty young thing, that was for sure. Those bow lips and the dark eyes with a spark of '*vitesse*' in them . . . and yet . . . why not? If he and Freddie could, why not the girls?

"I think you'll find the word you're looking for is 'patisserie', rather than cake shop. A cake shop is where me mum goes on a Saturday mornin', early like, to get the best and freshest rolls in London for breakfast. I wonder – you're more East End than West End, ain'tcha?"

With this epiphany unveiled, Ernest found himself stood more steadily and more erect than he had been for the past five minutes, and he had the look of a magician who has just pulled the silk cloth away with a flourish to reveal that the previously mislaid rabbit has now been found in his top hat. Elsie, on the other hand, felt now as though her silk cloth had been pulled from under her, and, much like the magician's rabbit, she didn't know exactly what to do next.

By now they were back at the bar, where drinks were poured and waiting.

She took a sip of her champagne, and giggled. "It does tend to go up one's nose, don't it? Bubbles, I mean. . . ."

And they both laughed, breaking the ice and any uncomfortable air between them.

"OK, the game's up," Elsie sniffed, copying the heroine from last week's matinee. "Phyllis and I go out about once a month if we can save enough between us. To be fair, we don't do much else. We work; we help our mothers about the home with our brothers and sisters. We clean and help cook. We both work in an office on the docks – secretaries. The money's all right, I suppose, but when you go to the pictures every week sometimes it just isn't enough to see the glamour and good life up on the screen, is it? I mean, you've gotta hope that it can only get better, and that one day you can improve yourself to a better quality of life."

Ernest could only nod in agreement. This same observation had been felt between himself and Freddie for some time, only from a chap's perspective. They both worked hard, and for long hours. It only seemed right for the lads to have a bit of what looked so tempting up there on the silver screen. After all, why shouldn't they? They weren't idiots, and could scrub up nice. So, it seemed as if both couples had been on the same agenda, just from opposing sides, as it were.

Seeing that the bottle of champagne was now finished, Ernest leant forward and whispered in Elsie's ear, "Do you think we can get out of here – the four of us, I mean? Let's go for a stroll. It's not that cold after all. We might even find a chip van!"

Elsie smiled. "That's us to a tee, isn't it? Champagne and chips! All right, I'll give Phyllis the wink and you organise Freddie boy over there. Mind you, once we're outside we'll break it to them that we've rumbled each other – or more to the point that Ivy rumbled us. OK?"

The 'OK' had a firm sting in it, and Ernest was well aware of this, but he was having such a lovely time with this girl, and he was willing to do anything. Freddie was duly whisked away from Phyllis, and Elsie steered her towards the cloakroom, where they retrieved their wraps.

"What's the hurry?" cried a bemused Phyllis.

"Oh, you'll soon see," teased Elsie as they filed out of the Tivoli Club and into the night air.

It was chilly, but not freezing. Ernest and Freddie were stood waiting for the girls, Freddie with a distinctly crestfallen air about him.

"You've told him, then?" said Elsie.

Ernest nodded. "Yep, and I've said he must tell Phyllis himself – after all, it might save his bacon for him if he comes clean directly, rather than if she finds out from you . . . if you see my point." He gulped a little nervously, still not sure if Elsie had forgiven him.

"Quite right too, Ernie. Now that we're outside that place, it is Ernie, right? Is that OK too?"

Elsie smiled at him and slipped her arm through his, and they walked along Dover Street, crossed Piccadilly, and, following the side of Green Park, emerged a while later on the corner of St James's Park and The Mall. There was a late autumnal mist in the night air, silhouetting the figure of a policeman as he slowly made his way along The Mall.

Ernest had taken his jacket off, and put it around Elsie's shoulders, noting that, although glamorous, her wrap was hardly practical in this weather. Freddie had done the same with Phyllis, who, after a short time of digesting his confession, had decided that he was too sweet a boy to let go of that quickly, so she would be benevolent to the cause. Besides, he had that look of a boy who needs taking care of – in a sweet, sensitive way – and she warmed to this image as they followed the path around St James's Park in the hazy moonlight, which gave the mist an ether-like glow with its own mystery.

It was at this point that Freddie sped away a few feet ahead of the others. He stood on a tree stump by the edge of the lake and serenaded Phyllis with 'Where the Blue of the Night'. As he warbled the words, not quite like Bing Crosby had done, he wobbled rather precariously on the stump, seemingly in some danger of falling into the lake. His long, skinny legs in their black dress trousers looked like pencils, not capable of supporting him and Phyllis gave a mixture of coos and squeals as he sang and wobbled. He didn't fall into the water, and hopped off the stump in triumph, fully charged and ready to receive the reward of a lingering kiss from Phyllis. He wasn't disappointed, and neither was Phyllis.

"Look at those two," Elsie said as she nestled into Ernie's shoulder. They were walking along at a slow pace, while Freddie and Phyllis frolicked ahead of them. "I'm pleased for her; she's a nice girl, you know. I hope your Freddie is a decent fella."

Ernie grinned and kicked a few dead leaves. "Yeah, he's all right is our Fred. Comes from a large family, but they all look after one another well. Mind you, they're not beyond havin' a few scraps – but let anyone else try and they close ranks in unity. No, he's a good match for your mate, I'd say."

Sensing that he was on a good line here, and feeling Elsie's warmth, it was worth the risk. "Would you like to go out with me again, an' be my girl?"

Ernie almost swallowed the word 'girl' as he said it, such was the sudden gulp of nerves. It was all well and good acting the lad about town, but, when it came down to the line, you didn't meet nice girls like Elsie every day – or at least Ernie hadn't. He didn't want to lose this one.

Elsie didn't answer straight away. She could see that Phyllis had already taken to Freddie, and there would be mileage in them – she knew Phyllis well enough to foresee this. For herself, there was only one question to ponder: what if Ivy hadn't been there tonight? Would Ernie have come clean at some point, or would he have had his 'posh fun', as they had unanimously titled the escapade, and then made a run for it?

CHAPTER THREE

By now, the foursome had reached the end of St James's Park, and crossed to Parliament Square, where the golden light from a fish-and-chip van beamed onto the pavement. There were a couple of people waiting, and a policeman stood chatting to the fryer.

Elsie had not said anything for a while, so Ernie suddenly marched ahead and ordered chips, tugging at Freddie as he passed. Freddie pecked Phyllis on the cheek and two-stepped alongside Ernie.

"Everythin' all right, Elsie?" said Phyllis, looking as the shadows on the pavement of the people waiting for food overlapped and intermingled with each other.

"Oh yeah," said Elsie in a tone of quiet plotting, "I'm just deciding on something, and not letting Ernie there think he's got everything fallen into 'is lap just like that, you know?"

"Sure I do," said Phyllis in the style and mimicked voice of Mae West, "but, honey, when you gotta squeeze, you gotta squeeze tight, right?"

Ernie turned round and watched as the two girls fell into each other's arms rapt with laughter.

"What's all that about? She hasn't said a word to me for ages, and now look at 'er!"

It would be fair to note that Ernie was smarting a bit at this point, such was his pricked pride, and raw, open emotion. It was, after all, something which a chap did not let out very often.

Freddie sighed, for Freddie was well and truly smitten. As such, he wasn't a great deal of help to Ernie in his moment of need, but he laid a hand on his pal's shoulder. "Hang in there. She's a great girl, and worth fightin' for. My Phyllis said so."

Grabbing the two wrapped packets of hot vinegary chips, Ernie smiled. "Oh, I see, it's 'My Phyllis' now, is it?"

Chuckling, the two chaps returned to the girls with their bounty.

"Chip?" offered Ernie tenderly.

"Ta," said Elsie. "Ooh, an' with lots of vinegar too, just how I like 'em. Is it just a chip you're offering, then?"

"Well, no . . ." replied Ernie. "I was kind of hoping you'd agree to step out with me, and be my girl."

He licked his fingers nervously, before taking another greasy, hot chip.

"It's simple for me," said Elsie. "I can only hope for a better future. I'm doing all right, don't get me wrong, but – an' it's a big but – I want better for meself, as well as me kids when I decide to have 'em."

Ernie allowed himself the smallest curl of a grin. "There she is, my East End girl! Well, isn't that what we both want – a better future for ourselves? Yes, you gotta hope for that, but it's easier if there's two of you to share the ride along the way, as it were. . . . So will you be my girl? It's one thing to go out dancing, and have all the posh fun – but for people like us, the hard workers of this town, it doesn't stay like that. We need to pair up, and that way we make our own posh dancin' an' stuff."

Ernie had started his little speech with quite a forceful and determined strong tone, but now it had diminished to almost a whisper.

Elsie looked hard into his eyes. There was sincerity in that look, she knew. All of a sudden, it was all going to be better from now on.

She snatched the last chip out of the wrapper and, giggling loudly, ran across the road to the base of the statue of Boadicea in her chariot, which faced Parliament.

Ernie caught up quickly and, grabbing Elsie in his arms, whispered, "So will you be my Queen, then?"

"Oh, go on, then," smiled Elsie. "You've gotta have hope. Now, come 'ere."

With that, and under the strong and defiant gaze of the Queen of the Iceni, Elsie and Ernie cemented their pact, a double act that would go on to last for more than fifty years.

4. COURAGE:
Jimbo's View

CHAPTER ONE

James had always enjoyed the thrill of a challenge. From an early age, it was noticeable from the twinkle in his blue eyes that if there was the merest hint of an adventure, a threshold to overcome or an achievement to make, he was there in a flash.

When young, we are for the most part fearless in our nature. As we grow, we become more aware of the pitfalls and possible perils that surround such adventures and epics, and subsequently we tend to err on the side of caution. A few of us – and James was certainly included in this count – remain fearless, opting to be driven by the rush of adrenalin mixed with the optimism that, whatever happens, it'll all be well in the end and make a great story to tell.

So it was that by the middle of the Second World War, James had made a somewhat rapid ascent through the ranks of the RAF, and with his medium frame and build he filled a uniform most handsomely. It was with the momentum of day-to-day routine that James – or Jimbo, as his flying comrades had named him – had taken to the skies in his Spitfire, and defended British airspace from threatening forces.

While many of his comrades had not made it through the war years, Jimbo had managed to get through unscathed, although it had seemed to him that the entire period of conflict had been endured with only the minimum amount of sleep. A chap took a nap when he could. Whether that was in barracks, at home with family on short leave breaks, or merely lying on the grass at the airfield in between sorties, it was always only just enough to make do. You very rarely got to have a really good sleep. For one thing, there was too much going on around you; and besides, if bells rang, or sirens wailed, you had to be up and ready for action in a trice. So no, the promised hours in the company of Morpheus were never realised – or at least not until much later on in life.

By the mid-1950s, Jimbo had been sought out to fly a new aircraft that was making a name for itself, the Vickers Valiant. In this he flew to Australia, and took part in some atomic-weapons testing at Maralinga in South Australia. This place was not known as 'The Fields of Thunder' by the Aborigines for no reason. However, it was – as it still is – a long way to fly, especially if you are the pilot, as Jimbo was.

The modern Valiant had that deeply rooted British atmosphere within its fuselage. Apart from the excitement given out by Jimbo and his fellow crew members, a combined smell of aviation fuel, damp canvas and vomit made a journey wholly memorable. Jimbo had a naughty sense of humour, and so of course stories told were of an equally spicy nature and origin.

Now, it was 1958.

"Did you manage to find some?" Dorothy called as she stuck her head out of the kitchen window and looked up the garden to where Jim had just emerged from his greenhouse with a small bowl filled to the brim with tomatoes.

He waved and pointed to the bowl.

"Lovely," cooed Dorothy to the children, who were sat at the kitchen table. "Now we can have a lovely salad for our tea, and with a bit of luck there'll be a couple of tomatoes left over for Daddy's breakfast in the morning."

Jim came in through the back door, and into the kitchen carrying the freshly picked tomatoes as if they were a crown sat on top of a velvet cushion.

"There we go, Mother! Freshly grown in our own back garden – marvellous, especially after all that rain we've had this summer."

With that, Jim pecked Dorothy on the cheek and distributed cuddles to the children, Anne and Robert, who giggled and squirmed in the time-honoured fashion that little ones have.

The telephone trilled from the hallway. Jim answered the call and, listening, beckoned Dorothy closer.

"All right, Paddy, I'll see you there tomorrow morning. Cheers."

Dorothy's face became suspicious. "What did he want? We haven't heard from him in a while."

"Oh, nothing much," Jim lied weakly. "He's got a small job for me – wants me to have a go in a new aircraft for them. Tomorrow morning, up at the same place, so I'll have to start off pretty early."

He tried to make it sound light and casual, yet Jim was well aware that Dorothy knew only too well what this sort of thing was all about. It was, quite simply, a fool's errand to try and dress it all up as something it wasn't – but he'd try.

Dorothy sighed, looked down at the carpet, then back up again and straight into Jim's eyes.

"I know what this is, you know – it's another of those test-flight jobs, isn't it? After all we've seen in the news, and never mind the stories we've heard that didn't get into the news. I thought we'd agreed after Australia, no more big stuff. We've got the children now – you even said so yourself; they are our number-one priority now. Then he calls up, and it's Jimbo this, an' Jimbo that, and before long you've agreed to go and fly the next darned thing for them. Well, it's not on – not this time!"

With an air of well-timed finality, Dorothy strode back into the kitchen, where she set about preparing the meal. She began chopping tomatoes as if they were the sole target for her aggression.

Jim stood on the other side of the kitchen table, and picking up Anne, cuddled her over his shoulder. He knew Dorothy well enough not to say anything just now – besides, she had a knife in her hand and he didn't want to go the same way those tomatoes were heading.

The small transistor radio was on, and to Jim the Everly Brothers were seemingly full of irony as they sang 'All I Have to Do Is Dream' over the airwaves.

Jim danced lightly around the kitchen table with Anne giggling away, and Dorothy slowed down her chopping to a speed more acceptable to the tomato in hand.

"C'mon, Dot, it'll be all right – you know Paddy wouldn't send me up in any old bucket of nails, would he? I'll do this one, and then tell him no more. I know you're right – we did agree the kids come first now. It was decent of them to give me a regular and, let's face it, a well-paid job after Australia. We both knew that it would settle us down once these two came along. But, Dot, just this one – a last one. Let me go up once more."

Dorothy scooped up the sliced and diced tomatoes and dropped them into a bowl with some cucumber and lettuce before turning to the table. She handed Robert a slice of cucumber, and he quietly began to nibble at it.

"Oh, go on, then," she sighed. "Never let it be said I stopped you from livin' your dream. But please, Jim, make this the last one, will you?"

She sealed the plea with a kiss, and Jim put Anne back into her high chair at the table, ready for them to sit and eat their supper.

"My dream began livin' when I met you – and you know it! But OK. . . . Now then, what have you done to my tomatoes!"

The children burst out laughing at Jim's mock horror, and even Dorothy had to allow herself a big grin at Jim's antics.

"Count yourself lucky that I kept two back to fry for your breakfast in the morning before you go – I'm not having my fella fly on an empty stomach."

CHAPTER TWO

The next morning was a hazy one; the dawn held a thin light in it which softened the view across meadows and fields in the countryside.

Jim, having been fed a bacon-and-fried-tomato sandwich by Dorothy, had left early. It was only just past six as he drove up the steep hill and out of the village where they lived, and before long he was coasting along in the car across the open landscape of Salisbury Plain. Here and there, the odd rabbit was sat in the fields having its early morning wash, and ears were flicking and twitching as they picked up the sound of Jim's car.

Jim always liked this time of day – the arrival of morning, fresh and new, full of anticipation. Summer was now taking her final bow upon nature's stage, and autumn was peeping out from behind the stage curtain, eager to see how many were 'out front', hence the hazy and slightly misty horizon. Jim sighed contentedly – this was a beautiful and blessed land to be a part of.

Memories from wartime flight missions swept through Jim's mind – dogfights in the skies over where he now drove, and being shot down over Italy, where he had been saved and repaired by a local village community before being sent home via the efforts of the Resistance operatives. He wondered how many had made it through the war.

* * * * *

An hour or so later Jim arrived at a set of large gates, where a young man in RAF uniform was stood on guard outside a small wooden gate hut. Noting Jim's car, and checking a sheet, he ticked off Jim's name and gave a salute.

"Nice to see you, sir. Go on through – they're expecting you."

Jim acknowledged the young man. He drove through the gates and followed the well-manicured driveway, which led to a collection of buildings and hangars, and an apron and runway, where what seemed to be the object of the morning's exercise was sat winking in the newly revealed morning sunlight.

There were some familiar faces – friendly faces, an oily one and a slightly nervous twitchy one. Jim had seen all this before – what he termed 'the welcoming committee', and after so many flights he was very tuned in as to how to read the overall mood of the group around him.

As with all things of a prototype nature, there is a nervous excitement between boys and their toys. A keen observer could be forgiven for watching this small band of chaps running about, giving Jim the full briefing complete with wide-armed gestures, and thinking that the gap between a bunch of excited and slightly grubby six-year-old boys and this crowd was not that wide a divide in the greater scheme of things.

The new aircraft, an updated and improved bomber, was to be called the 'Vengeance'. It was sleek, slim and, with the jet engines tweaked here and there, fast. Everything had been tested, tested again, and retested. Now the top brass had assembled on a viewing platform next to the old wartime control tower building, and were ready to be impressed by what Jim could do with the Vengeance.

All the pre-flight checks were done. Jim climbed into the cockpit, and now it was time. As he sat there, strapping and clicking himself into the pilot's seat, the owner of the oily face, a chap named Harry, was perched atop a small stepladder, and leaning into the cockpit beside Jimbo.

"I know you're up to speed with all this stuff, Jim, but there's just the one new thing in addition to all the speed stuff which I want – well, need – you to be aware of. This button here is for the ejector seat."

Harry's eyes darted between Jim's face and the control panel and joystick in the cockpit. The look given, like everyone else's that morning, was a mixture of excitement and fear. Jim, on the other hand, was calm and focused.

Harry wiped his hand across his forehead, smearing a dash of oil as he went, and continued: "If you need to bail, press this button here and the cockpit will open up, kind of peel itself away like, allowing the seat, and you, to then be ejected at high speed. Then the parachute will self-deploy and you can float down to the ground like one of them seed things the kids blow on in the gardens."

"Dandelion clocks," said Jim slowly and deeply, thinking this all through.

"Yeah, that's them," beamed Harry. "So now you're set to go – have a good one."

And with a smile that revealed twenty years of heavy smoking stains on what were left of his teeth, Harry reversed back down the stepladder, pulled it away from the Vengeance, and half walked, half scurried across the apron to a safe vantage point, from where he could see things happen.

Everyone stood back, and almost held their breath in excitement as Jim fired the engines into life and taxied the jet across the apron and down the runway to the end. Then he turned the jet around, facing the take-off roll.

"Sorry to wake you all up so early, bunnies!" Jim giggled as he took a firm grip on the throttle, and, increasing the thrust of the powerful engines, rolled the jet into its take-off run. Indeed, three fields away a small group of rabbits looked up and hurtled around in a spin for a moment before scurrying into their warren. Jim, on the other hand, eased the jet into the air, and, moulded as one, they screamed overhead as they climbed steeply above the airfield.

"Nicely done, Jimbo!" growled one of the top brass, and congratulations were extended among the excited group on the viewing platform.

The Vengeance was, as it had been predicted, very fast. This was the main selling point, so to speak, and already the RAF were showing it off to several foreign governments, ready to extend pens for signatures on contracts, which would make secure lots of jobs, produce lots of aircraft and, in turn, bring lots of votes come election day. The government had put a lot of money into the whole scheme, and the man from the ministry, with the nervous and by now sweating face, stood next to the top brass on the viewing platform, allowed himself to exhale properly and wiped his face with a handkerchief.

Jimbo, on the other hand, was enjoying himself immensely.

This new jet was delicate to the touch, and responded quickly and smoothly to every instruction which Jimbo introduced – the briefing before the flight had laid out what the brass had wanted to see and be aware of. Jimbo was going through the motions as required, and on such a clear morning as this now was, high up in the sky, he was enjoying the run.

Acting on a timed command from the tower back at the airfield, Jimbo swung the Vengeance into a wide banking curve and headed at speed out to sea, which seemed to him to show the Isle of Wight as rather a blur. After a certain time, he turned the jet into a steep banking move and headed back across the sea towards the coastline, which, although not yet in sight, was only a few minutes away in the Vengeance.

Then it happened.

Quickly, and without warning, the aircraft began to shudder violently, and, rather too rapidly for Jimbo's liking, began to lose altitude. Buttons were buzzing for attention, and all at once it seemed like the whole panel was lit up and blinking madly at Jimbo, as if to underline the severity of the problem at hand without getting too hysterical. Yet.

Jimbo checked everything as meticulously as he had been trained to do, and in a way for which he was so well known and respected. It was at times like these, when most people would all be hysterical and wondering which button to press first – or not – that Jimbo remained composed and yet, as in this scenario, firm with himself.

The jet was starting to go into a dive, and Jimbo could not pull her up. The shuddering and rattling of everything was preventing him – never mind the G-force, which was winning hands down. He could not regain control. This was the moment at which Jimbo made his decision. It had always been in the back of his mind.

Even if the chaps at the ministry and the RAF top brass had wanted him to act differently, he was the one in what was now quite literally the hot seat. His command ruled, not theirs.

So, accepting that land was not near enough to try and steer the Vengeance towards it, and in any case by now he had all but lost control of the plummeting jet, Jimbo pressed the button and activated the ejector seat. With a whoosh and a scream, the cockpit canopy rose up and tore itself away, and with a huge amount of force and noise Jimbo was launched like a rocket, clear of the Vengeance.

The force of the ejection, with an up-and-backwards trail, meant that Jimbo's last view of the Vengeance was of it plummeting and crashing into the sea below him, not leaving much to the imagination had he stayed in the cockpit. The speed and force of the ejection had been, well, a new experience. There was a small amount of vomit which Jimbo wiped off his cheek and flicked away with his hand.

Not since the war, and parachuting into an Italian olive grove, had Jimbo been in this position. For a moment his mind jumped to his children, and Dorothy. She'd be livid, and, for sure, he'd now be tied to the office job in the ministry. But there was no doubt that for the love in his heart and soul that he carried for Dorothy and the kids it would be worth it, and he accepted it without further reservation.

Now, back to the moment at hand – where was he going to ditch?

The sea below was getting closer, yet luckily for Jimbo, on a morning such as this, it was not angry or choppy. In fact, it was relatively calm. Jimbo dropped from the sky into the water with the grace of a mayfly, and he floated there for a few minutes, untangling the parachute from around himself.

CHAPTER THREE

He could hear shouts, and looking around he spotted a small fishing trawler cutting through the sea towards him.

To say that the men who pulled him out of the sea were excited would have been an understatement.

"Bloody 'ell, mate!" panted one of the fishermen as he hauled Jimbo onto the deck of the little boat, "We saw the whole thing – that jet came down like a stone. We thought you was in it until the lad saw your parachute, so we followed you – and well, here we are!"

"And mighty glad I am to see you," laughed Jimbo. "Do you have a drink of something perhaps?"

They all roared with laughter, and after helping Jimbo out of his wet flying suit they wrapped him up in a blanket and found a drink for him. The lad brought out some dry clothes, which, although smelling decidedly briny, were welcomed by Jimbo.

The little fishing boat chugged along the small estuary, coming in from the open sea, meandering between salt marshes, and presently docked itself on the quay of a small fishing town. Nobody seemed to notice the extra passenger who disembarked; and with thanks, backslaps and handshakes exchanged, Jimbo strolled into the pub by the quay, ordered a drink and asked for use of the telephone.

Never before in her life, had Dorothy been so happy to

receive a phone call from Paddy at the airfield. "Jimbo is fine, really. Down on the south coast – came in on a fishing boat. Yes – a fishing boat! A couple of bruises, but that is all, and they've sent a car for him. He'll be home by teatime."

Jim had barely got through the front garden gate before the door of the house was flung open. Dorothy and the children spilled out onto the garden path.

"My darling, oh – thank God," Dorothy whispered into Jim's ear as she clung onto him.

"Don't worry, old girl, that's it now, no more. Except perhaps if we go abroad on holiday, we could fly then. The chaps at the airfield were fine, and the boffins have gone back to the drawing board for the Vengeance – I gave them the rundown in the debriefing. They're satisfied with what I did, and at least the ejector seat worked as it should!"

Jim chuckled, and Dorothy tried to, but couldn't. She was just glad to have her fella home and safe. The lump in her throat was flushed down with a mixture of hot love and anger, but when Jim gazed at her, with those blue eyes of his twinkling away, she had nothing left but relief and affection.

The children were dancing around to their made-up tune of 'Daddy's Home' when all of a sudden they stopped.

"What's that smell, Daddy? You smell of fish – lots of fish. Pheeewwwwww!"

As they went indoors, Jim asked, "What's for our tea, then, Mother?"

"Oh, I don't know," said Dorothy. "With all this excitement I don't have much in. Shall we go down to the village and have fish and chips?"

Laughter and love filled the home, just as it should do, thanks to the composed and courageous mind of Jimbo.

5. AN INTERLUDE:
Meeting the Bandoolah Woman

It was coffee time, with biscuits too. People were sat trying to watch an old episode of some TV murder-mystery suspense thriller, but she kept interrupting.

It wasn't her fault. After all, as one resident said to their visitor, "Don't talk to her, she's mad!"

Nevertheless, Delphine, the lady in question, was somewhat stuck in a loop with her tale, so after about half an hour everyone knew the story.

"I have two of them, my sons – they're up there." And she peered just above the visitor's head as she spoke, raising an arm as far as she could manage.

The visitor whispered to a carer who was circulating with fresh coffee, "Oh dear – have they passed?"

"No, they're tall!" retorted the carer with a light snort of a giggle.

Delphine continued, talking again to what was a wider audience, gathered together just above the top of the visitor's head, her rheumy eyes gleefully squinting, opening and closing at intervals. "My two boys, and my dear little black girl, Phoebe . . ."

"A maid from years ago?" asked the visitor.

"No, wrong again!" smiled the carer. "Phoebe was the cat."

"All things black and beautiful, all creatures great and small," sang Delphine in a weak, thin voice, which had heads twisting away from the TV screen.

"She's got it wrong," snarled someone. "It's all things bright and beautiful, not black and beautiful! You see, I told you she was mad."

Delphine continued: "I can't bear cruelty to animals of any kind. So, the Maharajah said to me would I like to step outside onto the veranda and see his new elephant? I was thrilled, and agreed immediately. We all went."

Her gaze circumnavigated the room, yet you knew that what she saw was not this lounge on a Saturday morning, but perhaps a colonial cocktail party in India, just before the end of the Raj – when almost all the British were packing steamer trunks for coming back to dear old Blighty. A few were still being entertained for good PR purposes by the local royalty and high socialite glitterati, and it would seem that this was where a young Delphine was at this moment in her mind's eye. As she continued though, the lounge residents, visitors and carers all turned their attention away from the TV and grew transfixed by Delphine's story. It seemed that, after several attempts to gain the others' attention, this time people were actively listening to her.

"So there we were, all out on the veranda, and, my dear, there it was, on the lawn in front of us all: this magnificent beast of an elephant. Oh-h-h-h-h, he was so lovely, I fell in love with him immediately. The Maharajah looked at me and asked would I like to name him? I said, 'Oh, Your Highness, yes please. You MUST call him Bandoolah!' So with a wave of his bejewelled hand, the Maharajah commanded that it be so, and the elephant thereafter was known as Bandoolah."

Then Delphine finished with another poorly sang song, a version of 'Nelly the Elephant Packed Her Trunk and Said Goodbye to the Circus'.

This made some giggle, and one or two laugh out loud.

"Yeah, that's right – Nelly, not Bandoo-whatever-it-was!"

The visitor looked up from having done a Google search,

and showed the carer, now collecting empty coffee cups, the information online which verified that Bandoolah had been an elephant used in active combat during the war in Burma by the British. His name had derived from that of a Burmese general of great fame and strength. India, of course, lies across the Bay of Bengal from Burma, and so it seemed perfectly feasible for the story to cross over, as it were.

After all, as it was subsequently discussed, given the time frame based on Delphine's age, she could have been a young girl in India at the end of the Raj period; and if you were a Maharajah hosting a party, almost a farewell party for the British, who would you ask to name your new elephant but the teenage daughter of your guest of honour!

It was sobering, then, to smile at Delphine, who was just leading into her seventh chorus of 'All Things Black and Beautiful', and realise that it wasn't necessarily the random tale of a dementia sufferer. Some things always remain, and it follows that, for sure, events that are experienced with such joy, or indeed such sorrow, will always be the ones that last longest in the mind.

That afternoon, one of Delphine's sons, who was indeed rather tall, arrived and took her out for a drive to the seaside, and to enjoy an ice cream.

6. FAITH:
Working as a Double Act:
Pat and Arthur

CHAPTER ONE

It was commonly known on the High Street among nearly all of the shopkeepers that you did not, ever, either cross swords with or question Pat while she was out doing the weekly shopping. Moreover, if you happened to hear the bell over the front door to your premises tinkle on a Saturday morning, and on peeking through the plastic strips of your fly curtain spy Pat stood in the middle of the shop eyeing up the display cabinet with contempt and arms folded, you did not panic. That would be weak, and Pat detested weakness in any form. You put on your best salesman's smile, and strode through the curtain and out into the shop, greeting her with a breezy "Good morning. And what can we do for you today?" while holding her in your gaze – rather as one would a cobra.

If this method was applied, it would usually go off without a hitch. She would leave within a few minutes, purchases riding in her wicker basket on wheels, and you could share the tale of the encounter in The Red Lion at lunchtime.

People in general – that is to say, the majority of the townsfolk – regarded with amusement the comparison between Pat and a cobra, and would have smiled at the similarity and exacting perfection of the pairing. On the other hand they were all united in their quiet and caring affection for Arthur, Pat's husband of nearly forty-three years' standing.

As everyone would comment while stood in the queue at the

post office, how Arthur, with all his calm and reverent strength, could manage to cope with Pat day in and day out was simply beyond people's general comprehension.

However, they did not know the whole story; and had they done so, they would hopefully have displayed the same amount of tolerance towards Pat as they reserved for Arthur.

As is so often the case when we do not know the whole story, it is all too easy to draw a distorted or even totally wrong conclusion to any given scenario with people. This is always enhanced if we are not too fond of these people to begin with; then the flames from that dislike merely waft and lick the ongoing continued misinterpretation of the bigger picture. But then, we are, all of us, only human.

"Oh, hurry up, will you, Arthur, or we'll miss the ten past, and then where shall we be?" said Pat in a pleading and exasperated tone as she tied her headscarf tightly under her chin and checked her reflection in the mirror for any unwanted imperfections.

No – all was good. Now, where the bloody hell was he? She was just about to bellow when the bathroom door opened slowly and Arthur appeared, slightly stooped, and wiping his brow with a handkerchief.

"All right, love, I'm here. Let's get going, then."

Only pausing briefly to wrap a woollen scarf around his neck, and slap a flat cap on top of his head, Arthur opened the front door to the small terraced house they had lived in since they had been married. Pat marched past him and down the front garden path, mercilessly picking the dead heads off the remains from the late summer display of yellow roses as she sailed past.

Arthur took time to lock the front door and place the key safely in a special small purse he kept just for the house key. Then, searching about his person to find the most suitable nesting hole for the key, he walked down the path and closed the front garden gate behind him with a click. Pat merely shook her head and strode off ahead of him towards the bus stop at the end of the road, while Arthur followed behind at a slower pace; and if you looked very, very closely, you might have seen the smallest of smiles peek out from the corners of his mouth.

Even with strong gusts of autumnal wind, flecked with raindrops that streaked down the inside of the bus shelter, there was still a space between Pat and Arthur and the other people who were waiting for the bus. Arthur didn't notice it; Pat didn't care if it was there or not. It – or rather they – meant nothing to her anyway, and *they* were just glad of the gap between themselves and 'that awful woman'.

The bus duly arrived, and everyone climbed on board, shopping bags and dripping umbrellas included.

Pat and Arthur sat in stony silence for the duration of their ride, sort of looking out of the window. Yet, due to the rain on the bus's windows, you couldn't see exactly where you were that clearly. It didn't really matter though – they did this trip twice a week, every week, and the novelty of enjoying the journey had worn off years ago.

After forty minutes they got up in unison and got off the bus at a seemingly nondescript junction. Traffic was busy heading into and out of the large town, but you couldn't really deduce in which direction Pat and Arthur were headed. There was nothing around except dated bungalows, traffic lights and lots and lots of traffic.

This was where Pat had been clever, from early on. After all, the last thing that she had wanted was for everyone to know her business. As it was, she made sure that she kept a straight and focused look forward, while directing Arthur to do the same.

As the bus passed by them, everyone looked to see where Pat and Arthur would cross the road and head off to. What they didn't know was that Pat and Arthur, as they had done twice weekly for many a year now, had disembarked from the bus at the stop before the one they actually needed.

Pat had always maintained that, whatever the weather – and it was always on days such as these that she religiously maintained the sentiment – the exercise did them both good. Arthur would have happily stayed on the bus for the five minutes longer; but then, he wasn't going to change the woman or her masterplan now.

They walked across two sets of crossings and traffic lights, then over a railway bridge before turning into a quiet hedge-lined road where no traffic ever seemed to go.

A further ten minutes on they came to a set of high wrought-iron gates across a main entrance, parted and fixed in place by some elderly London red-brick sentry posts. The style was of a late Victorian nature, being both ornately decorative and darkly forbidding at the same time. Some of the paint, applied many years before, had now started to chip off, showing signs of weathering tinted with a tinge of rust. Noticing this, Pat tutted loudly, and with a darting look from her tired eyes she drew Arthur's look towards the gates as they passed between them. Arthur paused briefly, looking up at the curled iron fleur-de-lis patterns which adorned the tops of the gates, and, with his eyes running a bit from the cold wind and rain, pondered on how long it would take to take a steel brush to them, strip them down and repaint them. He'd enjoy that, he would really; but then, who was he kidding, at his age now? Honestly! Really! He looked ahead, seeing Pat waddle ahead of him, and he wondered, not for the first time, how much longer would they both be capable of making this trip?

CHAPTER TWO

As was the case with every visit, they were welcomed warmly at the side door to a long single-storey building, pre-war in its dated design.

To enhance this tired effect, there were faded orange curtains tied back at the corner of every window, and the sealing putty was a bit patchy on some window frames, causing them to tinkle and tremble in this particular day's bad weather.

Coats, scarves and Arthur's cap were taken away to be dried and warmed over a nearby radiator, and the care attendant asked, as she always did, if they would like tea. Usually – and Pat spoke for both of them – the answer was negative; however, today was different. Yes, tea would be lovely. Could they have it together, all three of them?

"Of course," beamed the carer. "I'll bring it in for you."

The room was neither big nor small, but what it was, no matter the season, was cold. It had stood the test of time, yet seemed so flimsy, with wafer-thin walls to the outside, that any passing hungry wolf could have huffed and puffed and blown it all down without a problem. As it was, this was all that could be provided and funded by the council, and so it had been for a long time.

There was a single bed and a bedside table with an angle poise lamp on it, and opposite the bed was a small table placed against the window wall with three dining chairs tucked in underneath it.

A high-backed armchair faced the window from the other side of the bed, and sat in it, twisted by age and paralysis, and spurred by bitter hatred and contempt for life, was Simon, Pat and Arthur's fifty-two-year-old son.

Anger without definition or perimeters is the most consuming, pointless, and yet most intense form of the emotion you can find. Without being aware of it, this was what Simon had fostered and grown with for the past number of years. He could not conceive or gauge the emotion, but he knew its fire, and drew on that heat for any required energy.

Along the window sill were a collection of things, all from years gone by. Birthdays and Christmases had been punctuated with gifts for Simon, which ranged from a once-upon-a-time golden fluffy teddy bear, now faded and in parts a bit bald, to a Rubik's cube, as yet unfinished. There was a faux-leather camel, a present from Morocco one year, when Pat and Arthur had ventured to Agadir in search of winter sun only to find upset tummies instead. As a result, they had stuck to Devon since then, opting for a week-long late spring holiday. A long weekend in October to see the lights at Blackpool broke up the remainder of the year, and was nowadays about as much as they could afford.

Arthur picked up a small Corgi-brand toy car, and, holding it in his hand, could remember back to when he had tried, and failed, to get Simon to play with it. He carefully placed it back on the window sill and crossed the room to the doorway, where the carer, Anne, was bringing in tea for three on a tray.

"I even managed to find a few bikkies for you," she said with an air of victory in her tone.

"Thanks, love," smiled Arthur. "I'll take it from here. You get on. I expect you're as busy as ever?"

"Oh yeah," sighed Anne, "but the day goes by quick enough when I'm busy, and besides, as you know, we're all one big happy family here, so . . ."

Her voice trailed off, and she averted her eyes to a corner

of the skirting board, even though she could feel Pat staring at her. She closed the door quietly behind her.

"Come on, love, you know she means well – after all, she's looked after our boy here for a long time now, since – well, since she was a junior!"

Arthur coughed, and poured the tea. Passing it to Pat, he offered a biscuit, which she waved away. Changing her mind, she took one. Breaking it in half, she dunked it in her tea, and then fed it to Simon, who took the entire half-digestive in one mouthful.

Pat stroked Simon's cheek with the back of her hand and sighed. She said nothing, but, as Arthur knew only too well, she rarely did on these visits. When asked why, she had volunteered the rare gem of a fact that while sitting with her son she often prayed quietly, and constantly, for some flicker of recognition, or even a few words.

From time to time there seemed to be a look in Simon's eye that suggested he knew his mother and father – but nobody was actually sure enough to to be certain; so perhaps it was best to assume the worst, unless you were Pat, who always assumed the best. She was sure that Simon was aware of who she was – and Arthur agreed, of course.

"At least Anne's given you a nice shave," Pat cooed, smiling valiantly at Simon, who stared into space and growled in the direction of the windowpane as it rattled in the wind. "We should say something about that – you can see he doesn't like it," Pat said in between sips from her teacup.

Arthur looked at the window. "I'll see if I've still got some putty in the shed at home, and next week I'll bring it up here and have a go myself. We'll be waiting forever and a day for them to do anything. . . . You know what it's like: budget this and budget that. We'd get nowhere. No, I'm sure I've got some left over from doing our kitchen window, so I can use that."

He was pleased to think that, unlike the front gates to this place, at least with this small task there was a chance for success. He wasn't entirely useless – not yet, at any rate.

Pat finished feeding Simon her biscuit, and brushed a few stray crumbs from her skirt. She stood up and went over to the window, where she looked out onto a now naked and dug-over flower bed, and she took a small handkerchief from her cardigan sleeve and blew her nose.

Arthur had sat next to his son now, and was going through the motions of telling Simon about the week in the garden. "Being autumn an' all that, it is time for bonfires, and trying to chase those damned leaves up and down the garden path." Then there were the horses, and he described how he had just missed out on a 1-2-3 last Saturday. "I'd have had a tenner if that chap had put a bit more into it, instead of – well, you know."

Except that Simon didn't and never would know. But, like Pat, Arthur had to keep going, trying to get some reaction. Besides, Simon was his flesh and blood – he loved him unreservedly.

'You have to have faith, but for how long?' thought Arthur. 'The simple answer to this is for however long it lasts, as without faith you might as well just give up and chuck yourself under a bus. That'd give them all something to gawp at!' And Arthur let out a short chuckle.

"C'mon, love, we'd best make a start back. We don't want to be out in the dark, do we?" said Arthur, the thought of the bus making him look at the time on his watch.

They stood up together, next to Simon, and, taking turns, kissed him on the cheek. He growled again, but they weren't sure if it was an acknowledgement, or just simply a growl.

Taking the tea tray with them, they found Anne, who was sat at a desk in a corridor writing up forms as if her life depended on it.

"You see? We've got to document everything now – everything. I even wrote down that you had three bikkies!"

And she giggled, which made her cheeks shine rosy, and her bosom heave up and down like a pair of bellows.

"Thanks, Anne," smiled Pat, tying her scarf firmly on again. "I know you've got shortages at the moment, but I'm sure it'll pick up – it has done in the past. But you know how grateful we both are for all that you do."

"Oh, I know, darling," said Anne. "I admire the pair of you for coming up here on the bus in all weathers, but it's what we do for those whom we love, isn't it? Simple really, but not many would understand."

With that, she put her arms around Pat's shoulders and gave her a hug, which to Pat made it all worthwhile. Arthur got one too, and he felt the true warmth and devotion from Anne, and it was this which helped them both manage the journey home.

Again, they walked back to the bus stop where they had got off earlier that afternoon, and in the deceiving late, low and fading daylight they perched in the bus shelter, waiting for the ride home.

CHAPTER THREE

It probably didn't help with the stark light shining from the street lamp, and the glare from car headlights catching them periodically, but Arthur and Pat looked cold, waxen, even jaundiced as they sat in that bus shelter. They looked at each other, thought the same, and said so. Then they held hands. This simple gesture was never done in open view on home turf, but here it felt right, and comforting. They usually did it after seeing Simon. It helped.

Presently, the bus came around the roundabout. Pat stuck an arm out to stop the bus, and they climbed aboard, but not before they overheard a voice from somewhere saying, "Oh, Christ, it's that terrible woman and her spineless husband, look!"

They ignored the comment – it didn't even deserve notice – and they were sitting down just as the bus moved off. Arthur nearly lost his footing and stumbled. He sat down with a thud.

"You all right there?" muttered Pat.

"I'll live," whispered Arthur in reply.

Usually it didn't matter, but today they could feel people staring at them. This, in turn, made the journey home drag on and on, so they were glad to be able to climb off the bus and walk off up the High Street towards the fish-and-chip shop.

Pat walked in, assumed her usual character, and barked at the young man behind the counter to smarten himself up, stand up straight and finish his words properly – "The Ts are on words for a reason, not to be ignored." After that, she ordered a large bag of chips. "And fresh, mind, not the leftover ones from lunchtime."

They were seemingly served up double quick, and were, of course, fresh. The young man wouldn't have dared do otherwise.

Pat came out of the shop, placing the wrapped parcel of chips into her shopping bag, and they walked home together, Pat in front, Arthur behind.

Once inside, the fire was turned on, and the living room door closed to give it a chance to warm up.

While this happened, the double act of Pat and Arthur, who, as the day had shown, had a quiet yet constant faith in each other, not just with their son, laid two trays for supper, buttered bread, fried three eggs and divided it all up on two plates together with the chips.

They then sat in their living room and munched away at their supper quite snug and contentedly, watching a young couple from Scotland display their extraordinary lack of education on a National Lottery general-knowledge quiz show. At least that's what Pat said, and she was, of course, quite right.

7. CHARITY:
A Day on the Front Line with Frankie

CHAPTER ONE

What he lacked in stature, Frankie more than made up for in character. His cheerful demeanour was always enhanced by a tuneful whistle as he went along. He was short and slim, with brown eyes and a very healthy-looking head of thick white hair.

On this, a beautiful bright and already warm early morning in June, Frankie made his way down the hill of the High Street, past The Royal Oak pub, and just before he turned the corner at the bottom of the hill he swung into a narrow alleyway which led to a kitchen and backyard behind a bakery and coffee shop. The smell of freshly baked bread and pastries filled the alleyway, and told Frankie that his pal had been busy baking since the early hours.

Charlie, the baker, looked up from where he'd been filling some doughnuts with shiny, thick red jam, and smiled as he heard Frankie's whistling herald his arrival. Charlie, perhaps somewhat stereotypically, was a big barrel of a man, with arms like tree trunks. He had short hair which kept a natural ripple of waves in it, and his pale grey-blue eyes were shrewd yet kindly. Together, he and Frankie were known around the town as 'Laurel and Hardy', but not to their faces. Nonetheless, the nickname was endearing and not mocking, since both men were held in high regard by all.

The two friends greeted each other warmly as they had done every morning now for longer than they could remember.

They had played football together in the school team, they had courted and married their sweethearts together, and Frankie had been there in Charlie's hour of need when his wife had died suddenly during one summer holiday. Charlie had returned the true call of friendship when, a couple of years later, Frankie's darling had been diagnosed with cancer, and Frankie had sat up through all hours nursing her to the very end. Apart from the regular visits from the Doctor, it had been Charlie who had dropped by with food supplies, and who had sat there watching Frankie eat them, just to make sure.

Nowadays they shared a morning chat and exchanged betting tips between each other, content and committed in the belief that one day their big winner would come in, and they could fall into each other's arms with a celebratory cheer and throw handfuls of notes around in Mr O'Neill's betting shop.

That day had yet to arrive, so in the meantime they thrilled each other with the element of the chase.

"So then," smiled Frankie, "what are we doing today?"

Charlie placed his twenty-third jam-filled doughnut carefully on a tray, pulled a small piece of paper out from his apron pocket and retrieved a pair of horn-rimmed spectacles from his shirt pocket. He put them on, and read the note aloud, as if it were the school report of a child who could do better.

"Emerald Harp, Epsom, at three fifteen; Happy-Go-Lucky, Doncaster, at four ten; and The Whistler, Ascot, at four forty-five. That's for you, Frankie boy! Destiny, if I didn't know better. If that trio doesn't get us a few quid, I'm chucking the towel in."

"That'll be the day," chuckled Frankie as he made a note of the tips and decided it was worth a go at O'Neill's – provided that the twelve thirty-one was on time. "We've got to keep trying."

Charlie wrinkled his nose in an overly dramatic expression of contempt. He twisted the corners of a large white paper bag, rolled it and folded it over before handing it to Frankie.

"Well, at least we'll never go hungry! Here's your lunch: two crisp rolls, cheese 'n' pickle, and a couple of jam doughnuts – with an extra squirt of jam just for you."

Frankie thanked Charlie, glanced at his watch and left the kitchen. Returning along the alley and back out onto the High Street, he continued his walk to work at the town's railway station. People around the town always remarked that even if you could not hear Frankie whistling, you could set your watch by seeing him at different times of the day.

He strode on, and turned into a small side street which sloped slightly downhill to a forecourt in front of the small and neat Victorian station building. On his way down the street, he paused briefly to drop a small bag by a somewhat tired-looking front door before continuing towards the railway station.

The large clock on the platform clicked as the minute hand moved forward – six forty-eight.

Frankie had worked for the railway for more than thirty years. He held the post of stationmaster, supported by a clerk in the ticket office, Gerry, and a young porter and general handyman, Wayne, who was unusual in his generation, being both keen and helpful as well as polite though he was still not yet eighteen.

"A real shining rarity," as Lady Kingston had remarked to the gaggle of ladies gathered with her on the platform a few weeks previously.

It had been high praise indeed, coming from her, but of course Wayne had blushed himself crimson and crept away to a parcel storeroom with the bumbling air and grace of a shy country bride.

Gerry had been on duty since the first train had left at five twenty-eight. He didn't mind these early starts – at least, not in the summer. It was always more difficult to convince him to do them in the winter though. But Gerry's Brenda always made sure with a swift nudge in the kidneys, which worked better than any alarm clock, that Gerry would be there for the start of the daily timetable, whatever the weather.

Having greeted his chaps, Frankie stood by the sink in their kitchen and filled a large watering can, quietly whistling away as it gurgled and filled up, rising in tone as it did so.

Then, with the full-on and regular routine and meditative mood he enjoyed at this time of year, Frankie went around the station, along the platform, in between hanging baskets, and even to the old and abandoned bath next to the bicycle shed, where his dahlias grew tall and bold. All the plants, be they wallflowers, Brompton stocks, roses, or basket arrangements which dangled over the sides of their nests, were an explosion of colour and perfume.

"Even Babylon or Eden itself would be envious of this display, Frank" – another of Lady Kingston's compliments.

With the warm weather, all the plants were glad of a fresh morning sprinkle of cool water from the large rose head that was fixed onto the watering can. Frankie liked this, as the water sprayed out in a wide enough arc so that every plant got a drink.

As he stood watering a hanging basket of lobelias and marigolds, Frankie caught a glimpse of a tired old front door along the street opening slightly, and Dawn stepped out. She retrieved the milk bottle she was expecting, glanced up and down the street, and then grabbed the bag next to the milk bottle and retreated inside her home. Frankie was quietly pleased. She had never known who her benefactor was.

For some time now, ever since Dawn's husband, Adam, had gone off with his unit on a tour of duty to Northern Ireland, Frankie had observed Dawn coping – or not – with the daily struggle of young motherhood and housekeeping. The nightly news showed difficult and very uncomfortable images from the troubled streets of Belfast, and, knowing that young Adam was somewhere in the thick of it all, Frankie had decided in his own small way to help in whatever way he could, without taking any noticeable credit. That wasn't the issue – it was all about doing something to help Dawn and the little ones. So Frankie had lovingly tended his garden and greenhouse, and a couple of times a week he would leave a bag of vegetables and fruit outside Dawn's door. In the greater scheme of things, it might not have been much, but Frankie knew that it helped – and besides, he took comfort in knowing that Adam would approve of his small family getting proper nutrition and vitamins from nature at this bountiful time of year.

It was June, and really quite hot for southern England. The weatherman on the news had been saying that it would get even hotter – and that would mean a ban on hosepipe watering, so Frankie was craftily quite glad that the watering can, and the early hour at which it was employed, could get through under the radar, so to speak.

Pretty much the same could be said for Frankie's fruit and vegetable donations for Dawn. She had puzzled and pondered for some time now, but couldn't work out who was leaving it all. The milkman had been interviewed and quizzed, but to no avail. In spite of this, she certainly wasn't going to let all these goodies go to waste.

Frankie let the last drops fall from the can onto some white allysum, and returned inside the station building. The eight thirty-two had departed, full of people heading off on the short journey to where the line would connect them to the main London line.

Frankie made himself tea, and not being able to resist, carefully uncurled a corner of Charlie's paper bag. No, he couldn't wait – and besides, there would be another one left for lunchtime. He stirred his cup of tea and clamped his teeth into the doughnut, which sent a spurt of jam across his hand. He licked the jam off his hand, and carried on staring at the brown envelope which had just been delivered by the postman. It had the railway company's crest on the reverse side of the envelope. Frankie had wondered for some time if he'd be getting one of these letters. He took a sip of tea, licked his fingers clean of the last traces of sugar and jam from the doughnut, folded the brown envelope in half and placed it in his waistcoat pocket.

'Click' went the clock on the platform. The nine sixteen was due any time now, so Frankie went out onto the platform, where he surveyed his small domain, and leant forward to see if the train was coming around the bend and into the station. He looked at the station clock, then at his own watch, and then again along the platform, giving a contented hum and whistle as the train came into view.

CHAPTER TWO

All of a sudden, there they were, swarming around him on the platform: young schoolchildren – dozens of them. The two teachers accompanying the group were trying to organise a smooth departure, but it wasn't quite going as they would have wanted it to.

Frankie stepped forward and blew his whistle. All the children either slowed down or stopped still, looking at Frankie for his next move. He surveyed the children and plucked three of them from the pack.

"You three are in charge, right? You have two minutes to get everyone on the train, or nobody goes. Get moving!" And he blew his whistle again.

Like watching a kaleidoscope of colour turn and change, morphing into more recognisable shapes or patterns, the three selected 'leaders' marshalled and squealed at their young battalions, and, shortly, all were on board. The teachers brought up the rear, and, looking down the platform at Frankie, waved and mouthed a thank you. Frankie raised a hand, and the guard on board signalled to the driver, and the train slowly pulled away.

Why is it that so many people in charge of large groups of kids haven't yet grasped that the best and quickest way of getting them all to be on side with you, or at least to work with you, is to delegate a couple of them into senior supervisory roles? This elevated position always has a positive reaction, and makes life so much easier.

Gerry and Wayne had their morning tea break, while Frankie marshalled and whistled the mid-morning trains in and out of the small station. The day was passing well, and there were no railway-related problems. Frankie felt his waistcoat pocket, and fingered the crinkling brown envelope inside. That could wait a while – he didn't have to open it just yet, even though he had a pretty good idea what the contents were all about.

Presently, and with the notion of going to Mr O'Neill's betting shop on his mind, Frankie was stood on the platform. 'Click' – the clock ticked on to twelve twenty-five.

There were a few people waiting for the train, not all of them preparing to depart on it. Miss Hinton was waiting for her sister – a weekly ritual that had taken place for a good many years, and the only thing which seemed to have punctuated the passing of time was the shade of colour in Miss Hinton's hair, along with her posture, which now took on a slight stoop. Nevertheless, as she checked her watch and switched arms with her handbag, you could see that she was getting excited at the impending arrival of the week's news from her sister, Alice, who missed nothing.

Frankie smiled to himself. 'That sister of hers could be a BBC correspondent in Washington, and she'd still get every crumb of local news and gossip!'

As his gaze went further along the platform, Frankie noticed a young lady stood right at the far end of the platform, right on the edge. This – to his trained and experienced eye – posed two issues. Firstly, when the train did arrive, the end of the last carriage would be past where she was standing, so her present position would be no good for a boarding point. Secondly, she was stood right on the edge of the platform, and this was not safe.

Frankie picked up his watering can and, quietly humming

to himself, made his way along the platform. As he got closer, he could see that she was young, hardly out of school, and of a slight and slender frame. Some would say, as Frankie did when seeing somebody this slim, "A mere rasher of wind, that one."

Her right leg was trembling quite visibly, and she held her folded arms wrapped tightly around her waist, with her thumbs tucked tightly into the corners of a thin knitted cardigan. Her eyes were fixed straight ahead, and every so often she sniffed loudly.

Frankie looked back along the platform. 'Click' went the clock – twelve twenty-seven.

"I'm sorry if all my lovely flowers have given you a dose of hayfever this morning, miss?"

Nothing.

"Are you heading to market this morning, or perhaps further on? You should move a bit further along the platform."

"No," she sighed quietly, "here is just fine."

Frankie knew that if she stood here, on this spot, the train would come around the bend with no time to stop before – well . . .

"Can I help you at all with anything?" he said, trying to sound as casual as possible.

The smallest move towards her drew a vicious hiss in response, and she spat the words back at Frankie: "You keep away from me, you see!"

'Click' went the minute hand on the big clock – twelve twenty-nine.

"Well," said Frankie in the tone of someone who knew what they were talking about, "if I were going to end it all, this wouldn't be my choice. It's not guaranteed, you see. It doesn't always work – or quickly, for that matter, if it does at all. Usually we have to pull what's left of the person out from under the train, limbs missing, blood everywhere, and then off to the hospital, if they make it that far. The screaming! Oh, you should hear it!"

79

"Shut up!" the young lady shrieked, drawing some attention from back along the platform, where Miss Hinton jolted slightly. "I don't care, you see. It's all over. We lost him last night – meningitis. I didn't see it coming. Neither of us did. He was only three. Now it's all done and finished with. I can't carry on. . . ." The young lady's voice trailed off.

Frankie placed the watering can next to a bed of wallflowers and dahlias, and, taking his handkerchief from a pocket, wiped his brow and dabbed around his eyes. He thought for a moment, and then fixed the young lady with a steady gaze.

"Are you telling me that after such a sad tragedy your spouse is left alone, without you to console him?"

She sighed. "Oh, he don't care – I think he's taking consolation in The Royal Oak right now."

Frankie grew angry. "How can you even think of abandoning him now? After the loss of your little 'un, you want to pop off and leave him with a double loss!"

'Click' – twelve thirty-one ticked the minute hand on the big platform clock, and the current in the rails began to sing as the train approached.

Frankie continued: "I can't believe it! How selfish can you be, you spoilt little bitch!"

She spun round, flaring with rage. "How could you say such—"

That was what Frankie was waiting for. He jumped forward, grabbed the young lady by her cardigan, and pulled her towards him. The force of the grab produced a loss of balance and Frankie fell backwards, pulling the young lady with him. As the train rounded the bend and swept into the station, the guard was surprised to see Frankie sprawled out among his bed of flowers with a sobbing young lady on top of him.

For once, Miss Hinton had some news to greet her sister with – hot off the press, as it were, and already burning a hole in her tongue to be told.

A short while later, and Frankie had brought the young lady, who by now had given her name as Chloe, into his office and sat her down. The policeman had just left, and a man rather shyly tapped on the door, fumbling with some car keys. This turned out to be Chloe's father.

"Take this with you, love," smiled Frankie. "Share it with your other half. It's one of Charlie's best doughnuts, and I don't give them away easily! I'm truly sorry for your sad loss, but go find your fella. He needs you as much as you need him – together you'll make it."

She smiled, and, still feeling not quite sure of anything, clung on to her father as he steered her out of Frankie's office.

CHAPTER THREE

'Those dahlias won't recover from the crush,' thought Frankie to himself as he looked down onto the bed of squashed flowers with a smile. 'Still, they did a grand job of making a soft landing for us, thank God.'

'Click' – three forty-eight went the clock. The train pulled in, and in a wave the carriage doors flew open and scores of chattering schoolchildren rushed off the train and out through the gate, spilling onto the forecourt. It was no wonder that Frankie referred to this train's arrival as the 'Locust Special'. Dangling half on and half off the train, parcels and shopping bags in mid-transit, was Lady Kingston. She was trying to find her footing, but as a shapely ankle and expensive shoe poked around in mid-air for the platform Frankie stepped forward and extended a hand. He was passed an armful of shopping, and received a beaming smile from Her Ladyship.

"Oh, Frank! How kind! What WOULD we do without you?"

Frankie felt the envelope in his waistcoat pocket – no, that could wait until tomorrow now. He'd get Gerry and Wayne together for the morning tea break, and tell them then. How they'd cope without him in the future – well, they'd have to learn. That, after all, is what they call 'progress', these days, isn't it?

He'd need extra jam doughnuts from Charlie to help soften the blow – dammit! The horses!

NOW TO THE PRESENT DAY TIME FRAME

8. THE VFR CLUB

As she listened on the phone, she was playing with the small, plain gold crucifix which hung around her neck.

"Yes, I know. I'm well aware of that" was all that she seemed able to say, such was the domineering force of the voice almost bearing down upon her from the other end of the line. Perhaps it was more likely that the subject matter was what the overbearing issue was really all about.

Mother had been on her own for four years now, since Dad had died. Things had been fine, and she had not even given the scenario at Mother's home a second thought.

"She'll be fine," they had all said at the funeral. "Time's a great healer, and, it has to be said, what with his illness, it rather tied her to the place didn't it?"

Why is it that people can be so thoughtless and insensitive on a day when they have probably promised themselves to be anything but?

Eunice looked at her watch and then in the hallway mirror, where she teased and pushed back a stray lock of hair. That would need tinting again soon – she wasn't as naturally chestnut these days as she once had been.

"Yes, that's all very well, but I can't have her here and that's that. She'll have to go from the unit into care somewhere. Don't you people have a list of these places or something?"

The social worker was quite flabbergasted at being counted

among the 'you people' in Eunice's question. She made some remark along the lines that she'd see what she could do at such short notice, and hung up.

Eunice replaced the receiver and returned to the kitchen, where her husband, Phil, was in mid-peel of the vegetables for lunch.

Leaning against the imported Italian-marble worktop that ran along the full length of the kitchen, as well as gracing the central work station, where Phil was peeling and chopping, Eunice took a large sip of her Pinot Grigio.

"Can you believe it? She actually wanted me to go and fetch Mother and bring her back here – HERE!"

"No!" exclaimed Phil, just a little overdramatically, although, had it been known, what he really thought was 'Hmmm, not one bit surprised. Saw this coming back at the funeral.' What he went on to say was "Good grief, the cheek of it! Such short notice too."

"Exactly," squawked Eunice emphatically. "I said to her, 'No way. You'll have to find her a home.' That's what they do, after all, isn't it? That's what they're bloody well paid for."

"Absolutely," confirmed Phil. "The bloody cheek of it!" was repeated for good measure as the carrots and parsnips went into the oven with a lamb rump and herb crust.

Meanwhile, halfway up the stairs Cuthbert, Eunice and Phil's fifteen-year-old son, was sat with his chin resting on his knees. He had heard everything. The lean and pale red-headed youth was confused, and yet burning hot with anger at what he was digesting in his mind. All he could think of was the sweet and kind Granny Elsie who gave the best cuddles, smelt of lavender, and baked the most awesome cakes and sausage rolls known to mankind. Where had that lady gone, and why was Mum being such a total cow about her own mother?

As they all sat and ate lunch in the dining room, Eunice was still fizzing away with an uncomfortable need to carry on about her mother. She stabbed a piece of lamb with her fork and waved it about while she poured herself yet another glass of Pinot Grigio.

"She said they had found her wandering about in next door's garden, using a Georgian silver spoon to scoop soil from the Baxters' border into her cafetière. Then she tapped on their French windows, and asked if they wanted amaretti with their after-dinner coffee? For Christ's sake, Phil, it was nine in the morning! The Baxters were having a continental brekkie before going to the tennis club. That's another avenue of pleasure cut off from us now!"

Eunice was not pleased. Phil didn't mind, or care particularly. The tennis club had been an expense he detested paying for, especially as he was so crap at the game. Eunice had liked it. She was mediocre at playing, but loved the socialising.

"Oh well," he mused slowly, scraping some burnt herb crust from his lamb, "we'll see if we can get in with the bridge and Glyndebourne set. That'll be worth a go."

Eunice smiled thinly, pondering the suggestion for initial consideration in silent thought.

Cuthbert just sat at the table and wondered, not for the first time, if he was actually invisible, and how much he really hated rare roast lamb, blood oozing across his plate, and with all that burnt – sorry, caramelised – herb crap on it. Why couldn't they do plain grilled lamb chops like everyone else, with Bisto gravy and shop-bought crispy roast spuds. That's what he had at his mate's house, where he went for his tea after school once a week, having had to stay late at school for the orchestra practice. He wasn't so keen on the clarinet, but, in truth, was quite good at it. So, if pushed, Cuthbert would admit it was kind of OK; and besides, he had fun with other members of the orchestra. He wasn't invisible with them.

* * * * *

Janet and Dave went every week to visit their father, usually on a Sunday afternoon. It was part of their routine, and also, as had been explained to them by the care manager, it was important that Joey was aware of a routine of some sort. That way, everyone knew where they stood, Joey included.

While this seemed almost incomprehensible, it was a help to Janet and Dave as it gave them both a framework to work around.

Janet would drive into the town, pick up Dave from his small and modest terraced cottage, where he had lived alone for some years now, and then together they would attend the town church service, followed by a fixed-price lunch at the pub carvery. After this, they went to visit Joey. If the weather was nice, Joey was taken in the car for a drive along the coast, and they'd all sit in a cliff-top café and have tea and cake. Joey liked tea and cake, and he also liked to look out to sea. He couldn't recall why it held so much meaning to him, but he liked it anyway.

You may recall for him why he liked to look at the sea?

Janet and Dave had promised their mother on her deathbed that they would look after Joey. Evie, who had been fighting her illness like a prize boxer for some time, had got to the point where she simply didn't have the strength left in her small body. Joey, who had already entered the early stages of Alzheimer's disease, was totally inconsolable, and unable to quantify anything in his world now that his sweetheart was slipping away before his very eyes. It was more than he could bear, and although Evie's passing was a release for her, it was yet another hitherto unknown dimension of hell for Joey to deal with. He could, and had, wandered from the family home just once too often, and the simple reality was that in order to give him the best care possible, in his best interests, Janet and Dave would need to place their father into a care home.

It had been draining, demoralising, frustrating and, by the time he was brought to the care home, exhausting for both of them. However, that had been a while ago, and they could see that he was content now, settled and well looked after. Joey lived for, and loved, his food. Every mealtime, he would sit at the dining table, neatly and expectantly, waiting for his plate with the excitement of a young child at their birthday party.

Other than the mealtimes, Joey would sleep in his armchair in his room, or wander around the home, seemingly looking for Evie.

Janet and Dave, after the initial settling-in period, were relaxed in the knowledge that they had done the right thing. They were always active with events in the home, such as 'cake bakes', biscuit sales, Christmas-jumper contests, and other fundraising activities. All this, if the truth be known, was just the right tonic and salvation not only for Joey, but for Janet and Dave as well. They felt included.

* * * * *

Jimbo's Dorothy and Frankie's partner, Beryl, had become the best of friends.

As they had said to others about themselves, "We had seen each other about the town for many years, and it's a shame we weren't introduced to each other before now." It had almost seemed a crying shame that Frankie had met Beryl so late on in life; but then, as they had said themselves, it was better to have this precious and loving time together now, bathed in the rays and warm glow of life's sunset, rather than to never have met each other at all. They had enjoyed lazy and warm days in the Spanish islands on holiday, and danced together with friends at many social events. There had been plenty of good times, and, if asked, Beryl was happy to say thank goodness they had done all these things together when they had, so that now, when it got tough with Frankie, she still had some happy memories to rely on.

Dorothy was a solid and dependable wife and supporter. Her Jim never wanted for anything. The carers only had to mention that perhaps his socks would need replacing soon and on her next visit Dorothy would produce a brightly coloured pack of six pairs of new socks for Jimbo. Both she and the two kids and their families were regular visitors to see Jimbo, and, in truth, they were all relieved that he was where he was, for it had become much to difficult to handle him at home and eventually the kids had made a family conference with Dorothy. Beaten by fatigue, fear and common sense, she had agreed that he should be given a better level of care than that which she could barely manage to provide herself. It had been the hardest thing to accept, yet now, and seeing Beryl every week, Dorothy was similarly relieved to be able to look back on happier times with her Jimbo. She missed his garden produce though, and would tell everyone that his tomatoes from their greenhouse had always been the best, juiciest and sweetest she had ever tasted. Then she'd stroke Jimbo's cheek softly, and tell him she loved him. He smiled back, and his eyes twinkled at her, still full of love.

Dorothy and Beryl were a great support for each other. On some days when Jimbo would just be fast asleep in his armchair in the lounge, dreaming of flying over the Bay of Bengal or dog-fighting in the skies over Sussex, Dorothy made sure that she had a chat with other residents of the care home.

This was how she had been introduced to Beryl, who was trying to make a quiet and discreet exit to the car park when Frankie realised her game and was speeding along at a snail's pace towards the front door. Dorothy had headed him off, and thereby had given Beryl the necessary moment to leave. Beryl came every day and, weather permitting, took Frankie for a walk or a drive somewhere in the nearby forest for an afternoon tea, or perhaps to the beach for a paddle and an ice cream. Either option was much appreciated, and on several occasions they had made a foursome, and the two ladies had taken their 'boys' out together.

Sometimes, the pain of watching your loved one deteriorate

and evaporate before you was simply too much to bear, so it was wonderful for them to have each other.

As they said, "We're in it for the long haul, no ifs or buts."

* * * * *

It had seemed a no-go situation, and just not an option to contemplate breaking up Pat and Arthur.

Never mind the budget constraints and the minefield of social services and welfare home-care packages, which had been picked to pieces by Pat, the simple feasibility of everything had brought about a move into the care home for both Pat and Arthur, as a couple.

Their son Simon had died from pneumonia "arising out of complications with . . ." and it had been here that Pat had stopped listening.

Pat had a sister, and there were two children there, a niece and a nephew, who lived along the coast not more than half an hour away. But they never came. Never. Not even for a birthday, or on Christmas Day. Nothing. Nobody came. The only post that arrived for them was the deliveries of items ordered by Pat through various shopping catalogues.

* * * * *

Miss Bridget, who had settled into the daily routine of life at the care home for some time now, was regularly visited by her nephew. Even though he lived some long distance away, he was happy to make the journey to see her every two weeks. As was the case with other visitors who came to see residents in the care home, he would sometimes be charged with a small list of tasks to be done, or a short shopping list of things which Miss Bridget wanted.

As was the nature of their close bond, the love between them meant that even if Miss Bridget had woken up in a foul temper she only had to see her nephew come around the corner into the lounge and her face would light up with delight and love, while twinkling away with a touch of cheeky cunning.

"Are you behaving yourself?" she would ask, leaning forward as if cross-examining him at the Old Bailey.

"No," he would reply, and Miss Bridget would sit back in her armchair and nod sagely, allowing a small smile to cross her face.

Pat and Arthur would sit and watch this small cabaret, as it would repeat itself every time the nephew came. Pat wondered if, had things been different, her Simon would have been this attentive and loving, and as regular a visitor as Bridget's boy was.

* * * * *

It was a few days before Christmas, and the care home was decorated and ready for an afternoon party to celebrate the Christmas season. There would be more celebrations throughout the Christmas week, but this was an introductory do, and one which everyone was looking forward to. There was a handwritten notice on the board by the front door, where other announcements and certifications were posted. A rather war-beaten but cheerful piece of tinsel surrounded the notice for the Christmas party 'for VFR' (visiting friends and relatives).

The residents had all taken a turn to stir the mixture for the home's Christmas cake, and when a ring came at the door there stood Miss Bridget's nephew, smiling and ready to entertain his beloved aunt. Just as he was exchanging greetings and Christmas cards, and taking his coat and scarf off, a tall woman, immaculately made up and dressed, swished past him as if he were invisible.

"Now, look here – I've come to make sure that Mother is settled, right? I'm not paying these huge fees for any old room – she had better be in the best you have here." The woman looked around the hallway and reception area as if it held all the appeal of a Turkish prison. "Another thing: I'm not paying for pads, or nappies, or whatever you call them. The NH bloody S can sort that out. Now, who's in charge of this institution?"

With that, she sailed on along the hallway, skirting around Joey as he stood halfway along, following the smell of food towards the lounge.

"Gosh!" exclaimed Miss Bridget's nephew to the member of staff who had opened the front door. "Who died and made her the queen of bloody everything?"

That was the thing with VFR – you never quite knew who would knock at the front door, at Christmas time or otherwise!

The senior duty carer smiled at Miss Bridget's nephew, her brow still furrowed from the indignation of being included in the description of the home as 'an institution' by that rude woman. 'Just cos she's wearing a bright and shiny expensive gold crucifix around her neck don't make her the Virgin Mary – she's more Mary Magdalene!' she thought.

Laughing to herself, the carer asked Miss Bridget's nephew if he'd like some lunch – or at least a coffee. Perhaps he could get his aunt to eat something a bit more substantial today?

9. THE CARE TEAM

CHAPTER ONE

You couldn't really argue that the job was boring, mundane or routine. In itself, this was rarely the case. Every day was different, depending on how people were when they woke up in the morning. Some, like Miss Bridget, would be snuggled down cosy-like in her bed, and would twinkle at you when you went in with a cup of tea. Others, like Joey, could be easily read by the look on their faces, as to whether you would get a smile or a growl first thing.

This generally set the mood for the day. That said, part of the challenge lay in changing growls to grins with some of the residents.

As for the routine part of the work, this was mainly set within the framework of the daily timetable. Due to the effects of dementia and Alzheimer's disease, a fixed routine always worked best for residents. Therefore, they would always expect, for example, to see the table being laid out for lunch between twelve and twelve fifteen, and then they'd all be sat at the table with lunch served at twelve thirty. This element, in particular, always pleased Frankie, who would stand in the middle of the lounge, glance at the clock on the wall by the TV and announce to all that it was now twelve thirty-one sharp. A carer would then take his arm and lead him to the dining table. He did this every day, and nobody knew why; but, you who are reading this, you know – don't you?

* * * * *

Diane was pondering what sort of shift she was in for, as she queued up at the checkout in the supermarket. As she edged forward, she mentally totalled up the cost of the contents of her shopping basket. One thing was for sure, you wouldn't do this job for the money – it wasn't the best-paid job in town. But it was a job, and certainly one in which you could have pride.

Even allowing for being plump, and smoking more than she knew she should do, Diane was an expert at handling the weight of a resident, whether it was in and out of bed, or on and off the loo, or (with the aid of a hoist) in and out of the bath. All of these tasks, taken so matter-of-factly in the course of the daily routine, required energy and concentration.

Diane reminded herself of this as she took a decent-sized bite of her chewy chocolate bar, walking up the High Street towards the bus stop with her shopping. Maybe in a former life she had been a Himalayan Sherpa, for that's what it felt like today. But then, the kids had wanted that extra box of Christmas cookies, and yet another tub of sweeties, and Diane couldn't refuse them. They were good kids. Then there was the 'little bit' of shopping that her mum had asked for, and which had made the packing spread into two carrier bags instead of one. It would have been easier to just leave that 'little bit', but given that today's shift wouldn't finish until eight in the evening, and she had swapped shifts already with one of the other girls, thereby forcing herself into an early shift tomorrow, Diane knew herself well enough to know that she just wouldn't have the strength or stamina to do Mum's 'little bit' tomorrow. After all, who would get the rest of the decorations put up? She liked her home to look festive and happy. Not like a dog's dinner, which is what the result would be if the kids did it all.

Just as the bus had come along the High Street towards the

bus stop outside O'Neill's betting shop, it had started to spit with rain, so the assembled group at the bus stop all mumbled in unison, pleased at the sight of the arriving bus.

Diane stood for the short duration of the bus ride. It wasn't far, but it would have been murder to walk with the shopping, especially in the rain. Even though Diane hadn't had her hair done, she tied it back in a ponytail, bound with a cheerful twist of red tinsel. She was nonetheless glad not to have forked out the money on getting her hair done for Christmas.

'I'll do it meself when I get home tonight, no probs.'

With that idea in mind, she got off the bus into the now steady downpour of rain, crossed the road and went in through a side door to the care home. One of her colleagues and the chef were in the kitchen, discussing menu rotations and, specifically, what they could tempt Miss Bridget to eat as she had entered one of her 'fussy spells'.

"It isn't like that with Joey or, for that matter, Jimbo. These two always enjoy their food, from the biscuits given with coffee and tea, to a full lunch and light supper. They always clear their plates, and either say a thank you or give the appropriate sounds of pleasure and gratitude – as much as Frankie will always, like clockwork," – here Diane and the girls chuckled at their pun – "be in front of the lounge clock at twelve thirty-one on the dot."

Jimbo would sleep so deeply, nearly all day long, that he needed quite a solid shake to stir him for mealtimes. Quite often he would jump to life from his slumber and ask, "Are we going up now?"

"No, Jim, love," the carer would say, "it's lunchtime, not bed time." But you know he didn't mean that, don't you?

Once got out of his armchair, Jimbo would be brought to the table, where he would happily enjoy his meal and savour every last piece of food. Not like Miss Bridget, and this was the present issue at hand which the chef was more concerned about.

"She won't eat anything green, and she won't eat much meat – she finds it too much of an effort to chew. But given her age, or rather the age of her false teeth, I'm not overly surprised. Perhaps I'll try her with a couple of fish fingers, a spoonful of carrots and maybe a small dollop of creamy mash."

The chef, Sophie, was keen for Miss Bridget to eat. She prided herself on her cooking – after all, everyone else enjoyed what she prepared for them. This had partly been the blessing of having had a French mother. Her mother had taught her all the fineries and delights of good French country cooking, and this had given Sophie the perfect start to her career. Now, a few years down the line, she prided herself on making as much as possible, if not everything, fresh for the residents of the care home. Where she was concerned, and having been given the budget by Mrs Richmond to do this with, she always managed to produce a week's food, including cakes, buns and soups, with a great deal of style, flair and, most importantly, flavour. This was not wasted, as ninety per cent of the residents, and all the care staff who also ate her food, were constantly full of praise. The food had such taste and variety in it.

Diane had often remarked that unlike her previous post in another home in the district, where 'everything was mass produced and pre-cooked or frozen' – therefore with little or no flavour – Sophie's food was 'almost bursting with seasonal zing'.

Sophie smiled to herself, knowing that the secret to all this was the clever usage of ingredients deployed from her herbs-and-spices cabinet. A pinch of a herb, or a shake and dash of a spice could lift a dish, and if – as she had got to know – the residents appreciated it, then why not? After all, as people age, their tastebuds and palate find it more difficult to catch any flavour in food, so Sophie's touches were a real epiphany. It made her, as Diane would tell anyone, a 'class act'.

Although short and lean – not the usual stereotype image of a chef – Sophie had a manner about her which when talking about food infected the conversation with the drool of saliva that follows when you are discussing the delights of good cuisine. She had an open face, light skin and big blue eyes, which were nearly always fixed to a 'kindly' setting in their gaze. She wore the standard chef's white apparel, with a chequered cloth cap, under which her light-brown hair was curled up in a topknot.

She had a small child, a little boy of four named Nathan. He was the true light and inspiration of her life, and she would readily and happily share stories with the residents, giving regular updates on Nathan's adventures and exploits. Between the hard work in the kitchen at the care home, and doing the 'other job' of being Mum, life was demanding on Sophie, but she enjoyed it all, and always managed to find something to smile about every day. Life was not for frowning, crying or sadness.

This very positive outlook on life had radiated from Sophie with the strength of a light beam as it reaches out from a lighthouse in the night-time. Other members of the care-home staff would always find it easy to talk to Sophie, and when she took a short tea or coffee break, and went outdoors to stand by the utility outhouse, where all the washing was done in large industrial-sized machines, Sophie would quietly roll a cigarette for herself and listen to colleagues' problems and confessions with the calm air of a village priest. She was by nature, in her character, not a judgemental person, and was not keen on labelling people. To Sophie there was no such word as 'normal'. Part of the zest and vigour in life itself is an appreciation of the rainbow of colours and flavours that fill people's lives. Therefore, she felt it was not for her to condemn or approve of any particular story or person as regaled to her by a work colleague. If it eased their troubles to share issues from their own home lives, then she was happy to be there, lick the cigarette paper and nod slowly while they poured their hearts out to her. It was, however, through all of this that Sophie followed a golden rule: she never gave an opinion unless invited to do so. After all, you may have the calm air of a quietly spoken priest, but you would never want to be seen as a pontificating bishop. Sophie was not 'up 'erself', as the rest of the care-home staff would tell you. She was 'one of us, salt of the earth' and carried other such endearing titles other than just that of head chef.

CHAPTER TWO

Diane sat for a while in the lounge, where some of the residents were discussing their 'Daily Sparkle', a time set aside during the morning when facts and important dates from years gone by would be read out from a prompter sheet by one of the carers. Left open to the assembled group, it would often happen that either a particular fact, date, celebrity or song would stir a memory from the minds of one or more of the residents, thereby introducing some lively discussion and reminiscing. As an exercise for the residents, it worked well, and even Diane herself was surprised from time to time, as she was made aware of a bright light from the past with a resident, just by announcing a fact or question pertaining to a specific date.

This time she had mentioned Fred Astaire and his film *The Gay Divorcee*, and how it had cemented his partnership with Ginger Rogers for a movie career together which had spanned ten movies. Several memorable songs came out of these highly popular movies of the time, and as Diane mentioned 'The Continental', Elsie almost kicked her brightly coloured knitted blanket off from her knees.

"That was one of my favourites!" she barked, and everyone looked at her. "My fella would twirl me around to that when we went out dancing. Ah-h-h, they were such lovely evenings we had together. Of course, I couldn't do it now." And Elsie sighed, looking down at her revealed and now withered and sad, thin little legs.

"Don't worry," smiled Diane, "it's still a lovely memory to have."

And with that she tucked Elsie back warmly into her chair and stroked the mad explosion of white hair which Elsie still retained, making her look like a lifelong fan of the Albert Einstein school of hairdressing.

Closing her eyes, Elsie hummed the tune, and fell into a doze aided by the stroking of her hair by Diane.

Jimbo was, as per usual, fast asleep, sitting bolt upright in his armchair with his arms folded and his hands tucked under his armpits. Every so often he would twitch gleefully, and you could only wonder what was going through his mind.

But you, you can imagine him thinking of a mid-air dogfight, or flying across the red centre of Australia, can't you?

Joey had by now completed his small sojourn along the hallway, and had planted himself in his chair at the dining table, ready to receive whatever food offering was about to be made.

Pat and Arthur were sat, glued to the TV. Both they and Miss Bridget enjoyed a variety of murder-mystery detective shows, and, to be plain-spoken about it, had little time for interaction with the Daily Sparkle discussion group. The fact that for this time period, when the Daily Sparkle chat would take place, the TV was switched off didn't go down very well with Pat, nor Miss Bridget, so they ignored the whole Sparkle business.

Instead they stared out of the window into the garden, where two blackbirds would regularly fight and squabble with each other for territory and a place on the bird table. Frankie and Joey had been put in charge of that, so during the winter months they would be wrapped up warmly every morning and they'd be taken by a carer outside, to place a handful of nuts and seeds on the bird table.

Frankie stood next to the dining table and looked towards the clock on the wall.

"No, not yet," he muttered to himself, and sat down next to Joey.

A moment later, he sprang up out of the chair and went patrolling along the hallway – only to him it wasn't the hallway, you realise that, don't you?

Along with Diane, Sue was the other careworker on duty, and with them, aside from Sophie in the kitchen, was Heidi, the duty manager.

Sue was a lady of slight frame, and yet within her sinews there was iron-strong strength of a physical as well as a mental nature. She had a short, dark chocolate-brown bob hairstyle, and flashy brown eyes which caught everything on her radar. With Diane, she worked well, and they enjoyed a good humour together. It made things easier, especially when there were more testing times with some of the care involved during a shift.

Sue had a large family of her own making, as well as having originated from a large family. They were all a happy band of folks and knew how to party, especially at Christmas time.

With the VFR party later this day, Sue was already in a festive mood, walking around with a piece of plastic mistletoe bouncing up and down, suspended from an Alice band worn in her hair.

Heidi was sat at her desk in her office, filling in online forms as well as sorting bundles of files and other paperwork. She sighed heavily. Heidi was not a fan of all this paperwork, but she was well aware of the necessity of it all. After all, with inspections being made at any time, and the general mood in the national press not being particularly kind to the care-home industry, Heidi of all people knew that in her position, she was the carrier of the can. Only Mrs Richmond was above her, and therefore almost all the day-to-day running and decisions fell on Heidi's desk, and shoulders.

She had been with this care home for many years, and, being a local girl from birth, was often familiar with some of the residents who would cross the doorstep of the care home. A very busy social life through her teenage years, which expanded on into her twenties, saw Heidi embracing adventures in and around the town as well as further afield. If there was a touch of rock 'n' roll to be enjoyed, and a pillion ride on the back of a motorcycle through the night after seeing a band in London, then Heidi had been the young lady to do it all. The red-dyed hair and it's spiky style had become a well-recognised trademark with her, and, even today, some of the residents would get a glimmer of a smile as if they were trying to process some past recognition of her. They might have seen her tear around the town years ago, or perhaps noticed her as she hopped on or off the train at the station. It wasn't a hairstyle or colour that one forgot.

She had known Frankie when he had been the stationmaster, and she had often seen Pat and Arthur out on their shopping excursions. Although she had not known Miss Bridget personally, she had known people who had criss-crossed both their lives, as well as streets and other local locations. All this meant that Heidi had a deep-rooted connection with her residents, and the bond held all the way through their time spent in the care home. Whether they left to go on to another residence or to 'go off and learn how to play the harp', as she would call it, Heidi was totally absorbed and dedicated to her second family, as she called them all collectively. She would always go above and beyond the call of duty – something which Mrs Richmond was always well aware of. It made Heidi worth her weight in gold.

The doorbell trilled and Heidi looked up from her keyboard. Running her hand through her bottle-bright-red and spiky hair, she looked at the time. She knew that the girls would now be settling people at the lunch table and helping Sophie plate up, so she left her office and opened the front door, smiling at Miss Bridget's nephew. While doing so, she peered around him to see a tall well-dressed woman stride across the car park in front of the home and march towards the door, ignoring the nephew completely.

This looked like trouble – well, a challenge at least. It was Elsie's daughter, and since Elsie had not been with them for that long it was taking a while to get used to the ways of this woman. She certainly hadn't made it easy for them, and therein lay the task ahead for Heidi: to relax the daughter with the knowledge that her mother was being well cared for. Heidi liked a challenge, and besides, as she found out moments later, she was not going to let it pass that this care home had been referred to as 'an institution'. That, for certain, was far too archaic to swallow!

CHAPTER THREE

Twelve thirty-one had come and gone; along with the other residents in the dining area, Frankie had settled down and eaten his lunch. Only two of the residents were still in bed in their rooms, both with heavy colds. One of these was Delphine, whom you could hear nearly all over the home, singing 'All Things Black and Beautiful'. Looking in on Delphine, and collecting her lunch tray, Diane smiled at her and wondered if either of her sons would appear for the party this afternoon. Probably not.

Miss Bridget's nephew had celebrated a small amount of success with his aunt, enticing her to finish her plate of lunch as well as to enjoy the dessert, which was rarely a problem with Miss Bridget and her sweet tooth.

Heidi joined Sue in helping to put a few finishing touches to the decorations around the lounge in preparation for the party, and Mrs Richmond, who had just arrived to join and open the VFR party, was cornered by Elsie's daughter. In a brief yet accurate assessment of Eunice's character, Mrs Richmond had no trouble at all in inviting Eunice to 'declare the VFR party open'. This had gone down well, and Eunice now stood next to the Christmas tree in the lounge, bristling with festive honour as if she were about to launch the newest Cunard liner.

Pat glared at Eunice with an air of total disdain and contempt – whoever this bloody woman was, she held no appeal or comparison whatsoever with Inspector Columbo, who was about to reveal the murderer in downtown Hollywood on the TV.

At that moment the TV screen went blank, and from somewhere in the lounge a loud tut was heard, followed by "Bugger! What now?"

Mrs Richmond stood up, having been sat quietly talking with Joey and stroking his hand.

"It gives me great pleasure to invite the daughter of our newest resident, Elsie, to open this afternoon's party. Over to you, Eunice."

Eunice could not have been happier, being the centre star of attention, and she declared the party open in a manner not unlike the opening of a summer country fête. For that matter, she would have quite cheerfully smashed a bottle of Moet et Chandon against the side of Pat's armchair. There was a deep irony in all this, and Heidi allowed herself to smile broadly and clap along with everyone else.

10. JUSTICE:
With Lydia Richmond in Charge

CHAPTER ONE

As she opened the envelope and smiled at the expensive Christmas card, signed in fountain pen 'in appreciation, from Eunice, Phil and Cuthbert', Lydia pondered for a moment.

He was a sweet boy, young Cuthbert, and certainly gifted with the playing of his clarinet. The residents had all enjoyed it, and since he had given them a short and impromptu performance of 'Stranger on the Shore' everyone had been pleased to see Cuthbert whenever he stopped by not just to visit his granny Elsie, but to see all the residents. He would sit and talk to Pat and Arthur, Pat having melted her icy exterior completely after a couple of Cuthbert's visits. Joey was happy for Cuthbert to just sit and tell him about his week at school, and stroke Joey's hand, which he liked.

Miss Bridget liked him, saying that he had 'good manners and clean hands'; and now that Cuthbert would 'pop in' most Saturday mornings, the TV was switched off for ten minutes by Pat in an expectant thrill for a tune from 'that nice young grandson of Elsie's'. Pat still kept a close grip on the TV remote control though, so the kingdom hadn't been totally surrendered, just a small section of the Saturday-morning cooking show was regularly sacrificed willingly for a bit of music from 'our pal Cuthbert'. That was it, pure and simple.

'Our pal Cuthbert' – he was young, yet so considerate and understanding. He had seen (and, in one conversation with

Heidi, had said) that when he came to the care home to visit 'the gang' he didn't feel at all invisible, not like Pat and Arthur probably did, since nobody had come to see them since – well, never, in fact.

Miss Bridget's nephew came. He and Cuthbert had got along well, discussing different pieces of music related to the clarinet. Cuthbert had wondered who else apart from the nephew had come to visit Miss Bridget, and on being told, "Nobody," was shocked. It seemed that several residents either had no visitors at all, or only a handful. He couldn't grasp why people who were connected or related to these residents just didn't come to visit. All these people here, at some time in their lives, had made a difference to others, whether it be their own children, with a decent upbringing, or their siblings – especially those with large families. Cuthbert was unable to grasp exactly why these folks were so often ignored or forgotten. It was wrong and it made him burn with anger, just as he had done that day he had overheard his mother on the phone with the social worker.

Frankie's Beryl and Jimbo's Dorothy both made a point of being there at least once a month to see Cuthbert play, and would coo and twitter happily to anyone who would listen, telling them all about him.

Cuthbert gave himself to the residents of the care home, and they, in their small way, gave him something back. Company, self esteem, confidence and an unconditional friendship. This, in turn, had done wonders for Cuthbert. It had helped grow and develop him into a more solid young man. He now felt he had a purpose in life and, unlike previously, was no longer invisible.

Lydia took the expensive and quite heavy card, shining brightly with glitter and gold paper, out of which were silhouetted the Three Wise Men en route to Bethlehem, and clipped it next to a somewhat thinner-paper greetings card which showed a playful kitten in a basket, tied in a big red-ribbon bow that read 'Especially for you at Christmas', and had come from Delphine's sons. All together, the Christmas cards were strung and hung in a line across the wall behind the dining table in the lounge, so everyone could enjoy them.

Lydia had somewhat of a pedigree in the care-home business. Her family had owned and operated several homes over the years, with this one, Pine Lodge, being the most recent and up-to-date version.

Staff had been given specialised training courses on how to handle dementia and Alzheimer's cases. The students had been given spectacles to wear which made their vision out of focus, or tunnelled, and special shoes to wear which made it painful to walk more than a short distance. Ear mufflers made it difficult to listen to anything, so in one day the carers in training had their senses attacked in much the same way as a resident would. This proved to be very enlightening as well as educational. Everyone who had done the course swore that it had changed their outlook; so, after some nudging and inspiring banter from Heidi, Lydia had done the same course herself. She was amazed at the experience, and heartsore for her gang if this was a taste of what they lived with day in and day out.

Taking off her glasses, Lydia stretched her arms up high above her head, relaxed them down again and took a sip of coffee from the mug on her desk. The mug, a tasteful blue-and-white design, simply had the word 'Bitch' printed on it, and had been a gift from her daughter. That had been hard going, but they had got there through the early teen years thanks to the discovery that Cuthbert played in the same orchestra as her Freya did at school. Since being introduced to each other socially, Freya and Cuthbert had become good friends – not quite an item, but maybe in time . . . you never knew. In the meantime, the unison of Cuthbert's clarinet and Freya's flute made delightful listening.

All things considered, it had been quite a year.

They had received more than their quota of spot-check inspections – seeming quite unfair after about the fifth or sixth visit. The home had got through that, and Lydia couldn't help but feel that Eunice had, in some part, been responsible for the spot checks.

Either way, they had come through unscathed and certified in good order.

There had been a few losses, with residents as well as in staff turnover, but Lydia had seen to it that a tree had been planted in the front garden of the care home in memory of all who had passed that year. Heidi's hair had remained bright red, and had seen her through a break-up, the loss of a pet and, finally, the passing of a close relative. How Heidi had got through the year herself, Lydia could only wonder at – she would have to see about getting Heidi to take some leave, but the woman virtually lived at the home, and, if not careful, could soon become a resident herself!

They had managed to get two of the large industrial washing machines replaced, as well as the TV, much to Pat's delight. That said, the remote control was now rarely in Pat's hands, since she was unable to work the thing. By chance, she had got her hands on the remote just once, and had managed to reprogramme all the channels, quite by accident, with the wrong corresponding channel numbers. It had been like sitting an exam in communications to untangle that one; so, ever since, Pat had been kept separated from the control.

Miss Bridget's nephew continued to visit every fortnight and entertained the whole lounge, and not just his aunt. Cuthbert kind of doubled up, and entertained them all with some music as well as sitting with Elsie. Eunice hardly came, but would drop in on her way to church once a month. Cuthbert, it seemed, was always unable to be there when Eunice came, and now Lydia wondered, and probably realised that this was Cuthbert's escape and precious 'him time' with those whom he now called openly 'my gang'.

Although Lydia liked, and was known by all to do so, expensive things, and the fine things in life, such as good china to eat off and lovely holidays in the Greek islands during the summer, she was at heart a homely lady. She cared deeply for her residents, and often could be found sitting with them, either sharing in a board game or just holding Joey's hand and telling him about her day, or the night out she'd had the previous evening.

She may have had a good hairstyle and colour, bright and colourful spectacle frames and a good fashion sense, but in truth all she cared about was her family and Pine Lodge.

CHAPTER TWO

She had come into the care home earlier than usual, as all the paperwork build-up had played on her mind. Lydia knew that Heidi had brought everything up to date, and had kept all the files in alphabetical and date order – an achievement in itself. Nevertheless, Lydia wanted to have a good run through the care-plan files, and make sure that the ship was safe and smooth.

She didn't always feel this invigorated to tackle such work – frankly, on a sunny and crisp December morning like this, she'd have rather taken her spaniel, Joe, for a nice long walk through the forest.

Lydia could wear her waxed jacket, wellington boots and a tweed flat cap, and look fabulous. Heidi could wear a flat cap over her bright-red spikes, and look – well, perhaps not so fabulous.

But a sleepless night had meant that, right now, she was unlocking her office door and Freya was leaving home with Joe and heading off for a good morning's walk.

Lydia greeted Sophie in the kitchen and noted that, yet again, Heidi was in already, ahead of her starting time, and that Diane was doing the rounds, waking people up for breakfast and checking that medication had been distributed properly. Sue was helping Pat to navigate herself towards the bathroom.

Lydia sat at her desk, switched on her nice coachman's lamp, and started to work.

In the lounge, people had been brought down from their rooms, or had made their own way there in time for coffee, Christmas cookies freshly baked by Sophie, and the Daily Sparkle, which was now being prepared by Sue.

Diane appeared with a more recovered and less sniffling Delphine, slowly making her way ahead aided by a walking frame, and giving the whole business the same visual effect you might have seen if Delphine had been the one going on her tortured route along the Via Dolorosa. As it was, eventually, and with a lot of encouragement from Diane, Delphine slumped into her armchair and ordered her coffee with two cookies – one for her, and one for 'Phoebe, my dear little black girl'.

"Oh, for God's sake, not that again! I can't stand it. Can't you take her back to her room?" appealed Pat to anyone who'd listen.

"Hey, hey, hey! That's enough of that!" barked Miss Bridget, who had just taken her dainty handkerchief and dabbed a make-believe smudge from her nose. "Don't you be like that! Leave 'er alone – she can't 'elp it, she's ill."

With that there was a bit of a stand-off, and Pat and Miss Bridget had a stare-out with each other. Sue stepped in, happily waving the Daily Sparkle sheet and trying hard to give the overall mood a bit of an uplift. It wasn't easy with 'All Things Black and Beautiful' being sung in the background. But Sue was made of strong stuff, and wasn't going to let this little episode take over.

"OK, ladies and gents, who can tell me about Table Mountain?"

She sat down in between Miss Bridget and Pat, smiled broadly around the room, and thought to herself, not for the first time, 'Some mornings, just some, is it really worth doing this sort of thing?'

Jimbo was fast asleep in his chair; Pat and Miss Bridget were full of thunder and venom for each other; Arthur was awake, but in his mind was away somewhere on a trip; and Frankie was pacing up and down the corridor waiting for twelve thirty-one; Elsie was curled up, dozing on and off, her coffee going cold and growing a skin on its surface next to her; and Delphine was now into the Maharajah story.

Then Sue noticed Joey. Normally, he would be sat waiting for his lunch at the table, but as soon as she had mentioned Table Mountain he had stopped still in the lounge, had seemed to focus his eyes for a moment, and then had turned to face Sue.

"Yeah, I went there," he said quietly.

"Did you really?" asked Sue, knowing from the history part of his care file that he had worked for the Union-Castle Line for some years.

"Yeah," continued Joey, "it was a bit overgrown with different African scrub and bushes, and there were them small rat things – not rats, bigger and more furry – that lived on the top of it. They hadn't long finished building a cable car that took you up to the top; otherwise you had a tough old walk up it, I can promise you that." He chuckled, recalling an image, and associated humour with it in his mind.

Sue was thrilled. "That's great, Joey! Did everyone hear that? Joey went there some years ago. What year was it, Joey?"

But, in the interim minute, Joey's mind, or rather the window into it, had closed, and the more usually recognisable Joey now sat at the dining table, looking around for any sign that his lunch was imminent.

Lydia had been getting herself a glass of water from the kitchen when she had heard Joey talking, and had quietly stood just in the doorway which led through to the lounge, observing everything. She smiled, wiped a small tear from her cheek – it still sometimes got to her – and was walking back to her office when the front doorbell rang.

She roared with laughter at the sight of Cuthbert all dressed up, wearing a Christmas jersey that flashed lights on and off all over a Christmas-tree pattern on the front, and was covered in a decent fall of snow on the back. Added to this was a Santa hat, complete with fluffy bobble, and underneath the hat a pair of plastic elvish ears. He had gone to a lot of trouble in order to deliver 'the look', and Lydia called Sue to come and see for herself what the source of all the laughter was.

The residents in the lounge loved it all, for they had become very fond of young Cuthbert. You could even say that some of them truly loved him, especially since he was the only visitor some of them ever got to see from one end of the year to the next.

He had just got started on a medley of Christmassy songs, which the residents were all tapping toes or hands in time to, and Lydia had asked Sophie to make Cuthbert a hot chocolate drink, his favourite, when there was another ring at the doorbell.

"Goodness, it's like King's Cross Station here this morning," said Lydia. "Don't worry, Diane, I'll get it."

With that, she opened the front door, and there on the doorstep, in a rather smart burgundy woollen cape with grey fur edging, stood Eunice. She glanced from Lydia to the empty hanging baskets which hung either side of the door, and back again to Lydia.

"I'd have thought you'd have taken these monstrosities down by now. It's not spring. I know I usually pop in on a Sunday, but I've got a form which needs Mother's signature on it, so I thought I'd stop by now, and I can drop off a small Christmas gift for her while I'm at it. After all, it's only a week away, and I doubt I'll get in again before the big day, what with all the canapés and hot mulled wine I've got to dish out at various functions."

She stood in the hallway, being scrutinised by Frankie as she shook some imaginery snow from her cape and picked off a fleck of something which had dared to stick itself to the fur edging. Then she listened and heard the clarinet music coming from the lounge.

"Oh, how nice! You've got a CD playing for them. That's very seasonal, I must say, and I'm sure it keeps them all quiet and pacified."

Lydia felt herself prickle and bristle. "They're not drugged lunatics in an asylum – or any other type of institution, you know." She had to get that in just for good measure. "They're enjoying the Christmas spirit, some music and their coffee. Nobody needs to be pacified."

"Oh, that's good, then," swept on Eunice, oblivious to any hint that had been made. "I'll just go and take a peek – they might remember me from the VFR party."

And off she sailed down the hallway, her cape slightly billowing in her wake like a galleon cutting through the sea. Before anyone could interject, she had reached the doorway to the lounge and stopped dead in her tracks. There, in the middle of the lounge, playing the music beautifully to a very captive audience, was her son, Cuthbert.

"What on earth are you doing here, boy?" She spat the words out at him as if there was a full stop in between each word. "Oh! For goodness' sake, what the hell are you wearing? Have you run away to join the circus or something?"

CHAPTER THREE

Lydia had thought that by explaining to Eunice what a wonderful thing Cuthbert was doing, and had been doing for a while now, she would calm down.

Lydia was wrong.

Eunice was electrified with rage, which fluctuated between the state of that icy-cold anger which really made one sit up and take note and the ranting rage which made no sense whatsoever. She said she had been betrayed by her own flesh and blood; she supposed her own mother was in on it all, but then, given how she was, you couldn't tell; and they, meaning Pine Lodge, headed up by Lydia, had brainwashed her son into doing their bloody job for them. . . . And on she went.

Eventually she stopped, took a deep breath, and had a large swig of coffee from the mug which Sophie had appeared with – trying and failing to provide some deviation.

Eunice looked around and spotted Elsie dozing in her chair, with Delphine next to her, singing and snivelling away.

"Get my mother away from that mad old bat this instant!" she shrieked, "and take her back to her room. At least she won't be open to any infection up there. At least I can have some privacy with her there."

The shrieking and raging had upset the residents, and Cuthbert was of a decidedly lighter shade of pale than he normally was.

He had been told to go and wait in the car while Eunice 'supervised' the moving of Elsie from the lounge into the lift, and back upstairs to her room. Sue had kept her eyes downcast, and had hardly spoken, except to quietly ask Elsie to lift her leg, or keep her elbows inside the frame of the wheelchair. Otherwise she dared not even look at Eunice.

For Sue, Eunice embodied everything which was so utterly vile and repugnant about some relatives, and how they viewed Pine Lodge. It was plain to see that Eunice had forgotten, or even had never considered, unlike her son, that this was more than just a 'home'. It was, as it advertised in the local papers, a 'care home', meaning that it cared. Eunice would do well to remember that – only, Sue didn't have the courage to mention this at this moment in time, not stood in the lift with Elsie being the only divide between herself and Eunice.

With Eunice now out of the way, Lydia and Diane, with some help from Sophie, attended to the residents, calming them. It seemed they were more upset for Cuthbert, so Lydia took him by the arm and led him back into the lounge, and sat him at the dining table next to Joey. Sophie brought another hot chocolate, and a small plate of Christmas cookies for Cuthbert, and placed them on the table. Joey laid a hand on top of Cuthbert's, and stroked it. Cuthbert cried a little until Joey picked up a cookie, broke it in half and offered half the cookie to his young friend.

Meanwhile, upstairs, Sue had left Eunice with her mother in Elsie's room, where Elsie was nicely tucked into her armchair with her colourful knitted blanket covering her knees and down to her feet. Eunice was perched on the corner of Elsie's bed, sat bolt upright as if she had been screwed into the bed itself. With a flourish from the arm of her cape, she produced her handbag and, on opening it, drew out some legal forms. She unfolded them and smoothed them out beside her on the bed. As she did so, her amethyst ring blinked and sparkled in the light that came in through the window. Elsie squinted, and gazed between the forms on her bed and her daughter. She smiled.

"So then, Mother, I need you to sign this form. I'll take care of everything afterwards, but I need your signature to get things going."

It had irked Eunice for some time that Elsie had refused to give her power of attorney, and, therefore, here they were now, at a point of some delicacy.

"What is it?" asked Elsie, quite innocently. Everything Elsie asked had a tone of trust and innocence about it.

Eunice instantly became spiky and impatient in her mood, easily fanned by the previous half an hour downstairs. "Oh, for God's sake, Mother!" she snapped. "Why you bother to ask I don't know. Just sign this form, down here at the bottom. I've got a pen here." She scratched around in her bag, and produced a pen, which she extended to Elsie, pointing at the line on the form.

Almost immediately, Elsie was not keen. She may have had problems remembering things – dates, people and so forth – but she was suspicious of most things her daughter proposed.

For one thing, she had never liked how Eunice had handled the upbringing of her son. Admittedly, Cuthbert had been somewhat of a late lamb, and this single fact had nibbled away at Eunice until – well, here she was now.

"No, darling," Elsie said softly, smiling. "I don't think so – not today."

This did not fit with Eunice's agenda, and she raised a pencilled eyebrow to let that be known.

Downstairs, Lydia was talking to Heidi in the kitchen as Sophie whirled around them, getting ready to serve lunch. "Well, she drank the coffee. Do you think she'll stay for lunch?"

Heidi pursed her lips and looked out of the kitchen window. "I wouldn't like to second-guess; you just can't tell with her . . . but, you know what, it may be worth asking. Shall I go up? We need to know if Elsie wants something anyway."

Lydia ran a hand through her hair. "No, it's OK, I'll go. She may be more responsive to me, as I'm the owner."

Heidi and Sophie both made a semi-low and theatrical curtsey to Lydia. "Yes, Your Majesty!" they said together, and giggled, unable to hold back their light mocking.

Lydia was used to this, and merely waved them aside with her hand; and patting Frankie on the shoulder as she passed him in the hallway, she went upstairs to Elsie's room.

As she tapped and opened the door, she started to ask, "We were just wondering, Eunice, would you care for some—" But the sight that greeted her made her stop still in her tracks, as it did Eunice.

The pen lay on the legal forms on the bed, and Eunice had by now stood up, and was leaning onto Elsie's small body, holding her arm straight up while she fumbled with a syringe, intent on injecting something into her mother. Elsie was whimpering, and wriggling as best she could, but about to lose the battle.

Lydia shouted as loud as she could, "What ARE you doing? Stop it! Right now!"

Eunice backed away at once, and dropped the syringe into a basin in the corner of Elsie's bedroom. She looked into the small mirror above the basin, saw her reflection and let out a low moan, which developed into a long sob.

Lydia knelt down next to Elsie's chair, so that she was eye to eye with the elderly lady. "Are you all right, my sweet? I think we should get the Doctor out to have a look at you, just to be safe." She stroked Elsie's mad explosion of white hair softly as she spoke to her.

Elsie paused for a moment, and then smiled and said, "Yes, dear, whatever you say."

Putting on a pair of purple medical gloves, Lydia picked the syringe out of the basin, noticed that it was empty and stood in front of Eunice, for the first time holding a form of moral high ground. "I think you and I need to have a little chat in my office, and you will be staying for lunch."

Eunice wrapped herself in her cape, picked up the forms, took half a step towards her mother and then thought twice about it. Instead, she left the room and went downstairs to the office, with Lydia following her like a prison guard.

CHAPTER FOUR

They sat in Lydia's office in silence for a short while. Lydia had placed the empty syringe on her desk. Eunice had cried quietly for a while, but was now wiping her eyes and blowing her nose.

"I suppose you think I'm the worst daughter ever," sighed Eunice, "but, really, I needed to get her signature today. When she said no, I just thought about my plan B; and at least an embolism would have been quick, and at her age a Doctor would not have been so surprised." With that offloaded, she cried a bit more.

Lydia sighed. She had already called in Dr Matthew Raven, who was the main practitioner to most of the residents. He was young, tanned, handsome, with green eyes and sandy hair. The carers, and even Sophie, ranked him as 'the tastiest GP in town'; and if he was due, there was always a rush to answer the front door. His appeal also had a charm reaction with the residents. Pat became coquettish and flirty, Miss Bridget would just blush, and Elsie giggled. To his credit, Matthew Raven took it all in his stride, and always made a little extra time to chat with his patients whenever he visited Pine Lodge.

He had checked Elsie, and her arm. Apart from being a little shaken, she was fine, and Matthew stayed a few minutes to chat with her. Once she was giggling, he felt comfortable enough to leave.

Lydia had pretty much decided that if Matthew had said

Elsie needed a trip to the hospital, then she would have had to get the police involved with Eunice, and it would have all got ugly, and in the papers – or even, God forbid, on the local TV evening news. Then Pine Lodge would have had to close, and the residents would have been relocated, and . . . No, not this – it wasn't an option now.

She felt comfortable enough to handle this in her own way, so she spoke to Eunice: "Don't you realise that you're not the only relative with worries, fears and even resentment issues? The diseases which affect our residents are bad enough, but the cruel cheating that it eventually wreaks on the relatives and friends of our residents often means that they become neglectful out of no other reason than fear. There are, of course, a few exceptions. Cuthbert is a rarity, in so far as for someone so young he is simply amazing with all the residents. It is just so touching the way he interacts with them all, and they absolutely adore him. You could do worse things than take a leaf out of his book."

Eunice looked at the floor. "I just never knew how good Cuthbert was – I didn't even know he was that good with the clarinet." And she began to cry again.

Lydia passed her a box of tissues.

"He plays in the school orchestra with my daughter Freya, and they even give little concerts here together – they're a huge hit."

Eunice looked surprised. "I knew he played in the orchestra, but thought it was just a diversion for those teen-year-type things – not that he was actually any good at it. My mother was always good with him, even when he was a wee tot, and they shared a connection that I felt I had never had."

"Well," said Lydia, "I think you should start to try and get that connection going – not just with Cuthbert, but try to spend a bit more time with your mother. She needs you. Besides, she did a good job bringing you up, didn't she?"

"Oh, most definitely," admitted Eunice. "Both she and my

father made many sacrifices to make sure that I had the best education and nice things at home. I've let her down now."

Lydia stood up. "Not yet you haven't. Go into the lounge – Cuthbert is there with Joey and Jimbo. I dare say Jimbo will be asleep; but if not, he and Cuthbert will be talking about planes. Joey is just happy to be near to Cuthbert. Then there's Pat and Arthur – nobody else comes to see them, ever. Cuthbert is the only one who bothers with them. Delphine may be stuck in a loop with her story and songs, but he listens and chats, even if she doesn't interact that much with him."

Just to be on the safe side, Lydia placed the syringe in her desk drawer and locked it. She may have been feeling seasonally benevolent, and keen to protect her beloved Pine Lodge and its residents, but she wasn't stupid.

An hour later, and Eunice was sat with Cuthbert in the lounge, having lunch. She couldn't believe the flavour that Sophie had infused into the fish cakes, and Cuthbert, although a little nervous, was happy to have his mum there. Elsie was asleep in her room, and would be fine after a good night's sleep.

Lydia and Heidi were in the kitchen, and Sophie asked how many would be coming for the Christmas Day lunch – and Lydia had to say this year there'd be an extra two.